Giulia

CARA DRISCOLL

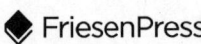 FriesenPress

Suite 300 - 990 Fort St
Victoria, BC, V8V 3K2
Canada

www.friesenpress.com

Copyright © 2021 by Cara G Driscoll
First Edition — 2021

All rights reserved.

This story is a work of fiction based on the author's extensive reading of Giulia, her family and women during Roman times. Giulia's unfinished story was discovered when researching women that would be formed into clay vessels. Many of the characters in this story are taken from the bible and from historical records. The characters and events are a result of the author's dramatization of the historical account. Although many sources of inspiration are cited and credited, such references are not to be taken as sources of fact. Details in the book are fictional renditions of the author's imagination.

No part of this publication may be reproduced in any form, or by any means, electronic or mechanical, including photocopying, recording, or any information browsing, storage, or retrieval system, without permission in writing from FriesenPress.

ISBN
978-1-5255-8950-8 (Hardcover)
978-1-5255-8949-2 (Paperback)
978-1-5255-8951-5 (eBook)

1. FICTION, HISTORICAL, ANCIENT

Distributed to the trade by The Ingram Book Company

*For Rhonda
A precious daughter*

SYNOPSIS

The year is 2 B.C. Giulia, the daughter of Caesar Augustus and his former wife Scribonia, has been exiled to the island of Pandateria for five years for her licentious behaviour. At the hearing, Giulia has also been divorced from her third husband, Tiberius. Tiberius is the son of Caesar Augustus' wife Livia. The union of Tiberius and Giulia was meant to strengthen the empire.

The story of exile is woven together with historical facts and imagination. It takes place during the time of transition from acquiring land to build the Roman Empire to the implementation of the *Pax Romana*.

Giulia's behaviour was contrary to the higher moral standards that her father, Caesar Augustus was attempting to implement. Giulia is traumatized by the experience of exile. Being removed from all that is familiar is an agonizing slow process that moves her from shock to a subtle transformation.

The theme focuses on the 'outside the camp' experience. The characters give voice to those aliens who are shunned, estranged, exiled or forgotten. It is a story of their transformation and the resilience of the human spirit.

The characters:

Giulia – a woman of the gens, descendent of the clan Julius.

Damaris – whose name means "heifer". Damaris became lame after her foot was trampled by a Roman soldier. She was Livia's servant and is sent into exile to report on Giulia. In addition, her lameness is seen as a bad omen for the emperor's household. Damaris becomes the stabilizing force for the exiles.

Mishma – whose name means "one who hears". Mishma was sent into exile because of his foul odour from a botched operation after being made a eunuch. After serving for five years he will become a libertine. Mishma struggles with coming to terms with his loss of manhood.

Dilf – Whose name derives from Delphinium and means "Buttercup". Dilf's father indentured her for five years' service in lieu of taxes owing to the Roman Empire. Dilf has served two years. She will become a libertine after serving for three more years. She has agreed to go into exile because Damaris, whom she admires, has requested her service. Dilf desires to be useful.

Claudia – whose name means "lame". Claudia joins the exiles later in their exile. She plays a pivotal role in bringing them hope. She helps each character become aware of their inherent wisdom.

Names during these times carried significance. To know a person's name provides insights into their character. Sometimes, women during these times were referred to as someone's wife or mother or their place of origin, for example: "Pontius Pilate's Wife"," Lot's Wife" or the "Samaritan Woman at the Well". Their stories often went unfinished which leads to speculation or imagination to fill in the missing blanks. I depended on accounts of Caesar Augustus and Tiberius to research Giulia's story.

Giulia's story is based on these ideas. Symbolism, such as salt and eagles, plays an important role.

DISCLAIMER

This story is a work of fiction based on the author's extensive reading on women during biblical times. For ten years I gave voice to women of the bible by giving them form in the shape of figurative clay vessels. I discovered Giulia's unfinished story when researching "Pontius Pilate's Wife".

Many of the characters are taken from historical records. The characters and events are a result of the author's dramatization of the historical account.

Although many sources of inspiration are cited and credited, such references are not to be taken as sources of fact.

Details in the book are fictional renditions of the author's imagination.

* * * * * * * * *

Author: Cara Driscoll is an artist residing in Regina. Intricately hand-coiling in the shape of figurative vessels, make her work identifiable. While the clay is still wet, text is inscribed in the bottom of the vessel which reveals or conceals something about the character being depicted.

A ten year project gave voice to women of the bible by forming them into clay vessels. The project lead to facilitating retreats and giving presentations on the "Forgotten Women of the Bible". The series began with an interest in literary characters. Another exhibition titled "Memory in Clay" focused on the historical aspect of the material used to create the vessels.

For ten years I have strived to give Giulia a voice by shaping her story into words.

Cara graduated in 1991 from the University of Regina with a major in visual arts. In 2010 she completed the Prairie Jubilee Spiritual Formation Program based out of the University of Winnipeg. The connection between art and spirituality is the focus of her work.

Website: www.caradriscoll.ca

"Oh Liberty, What Things are Done in Thy Name"
(unknown)

I

How quickly a dream evaporates! In the dream, I was offered some choices and I chose 'March'. That is all I can recall from the dream.

With one eye shut fast to my face, I awake, writhing in pain from a severe cramp in my leg. I need to relieve the agony, but I cannot move my head. My hair is effectively adhered to my pillow. My left breast is squished under my armpit, causing more discomfort. I am unable to turn over to release my breast from its prison. My head is heavy laden with the burden of regret. Yanking my hair free, I lean over the side of the bed. I cry out in pain and turn my head away from the putrid smell of stale vomit, which I know full well is my own. In disgust, I turn my head away from this blatant reminder of last night's folly. I try and recall where I have been and what I have done, but the memory is as elusive as the dream.

My tongue is thick as felted wool and my skin is sensitive to touch. Everything hurts. I cry out for Phoebe to bring some water, shocked by a raspy voice I hardly recognize as my own. I need water for my parched throat, water to wash away this rancid smell coming from my own body, and water to open my left eye. My cries for Phoebe go unanswered. Instead, Damaris, Livia's servant responds to my calls. I note Phoebe's absence but am too weak to question it.

Damaris pulls back the curtain, almost renting them in two. The bright morning sun pierces my eyes. I motion with wagging fingers for Damaris to close them again. She ignores my order. "Just water," I mumble. I am not ready to talk, never mind argue.

"Wake up, wake up, you must get up immediately," Damaris exclaims. I lean forward slowly. On the floor beside my bed is a pool of curdled pink fluid hinting of red wine that has lost its boldness, embedded with little bits of lamb, grapes, olives, eggs, figs and regret. The grim reminders of last night lay close to the bedpan, but not in it. On wobbly legs and as quickly as possible,

I make my way to the toilet. My urine stinks with the astringent odour of asparagus. I cover my nose in disgust.

"Please bring me more water," I plead.

"Giulia," Damaris exclaims, "You have been summoned by your father to go immediately to the Praetorium. We must make you presentable." Damaris' hands shake visibly as she lays out the preparations for my morning ablutions. Beads of perspiration form on my own brow. Then, just as suddenly as if in congruence with the prickly situation, chills run down my spine.

The dissonant shuffle of Damaris' footsteps magnifies the tension in the room. I cannot think clearly with all this distraction.

I ask Damaris to bring me my mirror. Baggy swollen eyes smudged with black kohl peer back at me. The puffy skin on my face is imprinted with the folds of my pillow. Wilted flowers and limp curls, hold nothing of the previous splendour of my dressed hair. The reflection bears scant resemblance to the dignified and confident image of yesterday. It is evident that the brass mirror needs polishing! I look towards Damaris and utter a whimpered cry for help.

Damaris springs into action and brings water for me to drink, which I quickly throw up producing only salty bile. The crust which has glued my eyes shut finally dissipates with the help of hot cloths. Nervously, I survey my surroundings with darting eye movements, coaxing the room to offer some clue for a solution. The corners of the room speak eloquently of my entrapment, while the marble walls belie its indifference.

I tear off my own clothing. Damaris' slow motions are not in keeping with this sudden sense of urgency. I am used to Phoebe's efficiency, or perhaps it is just that she is used to my impatience. I splash cold water on my face. Damaris brings the onyx box that holds the women's colours. Deciding against them, I pinch my cheeks to give them colour. I wince with pain.

"My skin hurts." I whine, but Damaris does not give me the sympathy I hope for.

Then I change my mind, recalling the reflection in that deceitful mirror. I allow Damaris to add a hint of black kohl liner to the eyelids, coconut oil to my lips, and just a slight dusting of red iron oxide to my cheeks. Damaris combs little scabs of dried vomit out of my hair. Livia's servant is doing her best with the mess that was once a vision of fine craftsmanship taking Phoebe three hours to plait and primp. It now resembles a dry hay stack. I try to be more patient with Damaris. It would take several hours under normal circumstances to remove all the pins and combs and hairpieces while carefully combing out the lacquered strands. Damaris pulls back the entire mass and ties it with a silk scarf while I smooth some wisps of wayward hair and fasten them with an ivory comb gifted to me by my father on my 12th birthday. The comb is inscribed with the words 'Modistina', likely a sign of his aspirations for me. Feelings of sadness and shame wash over me as I finger the words inscribed on the comb.

Just a few hours ago, we were all so witty and charming, filled with merriment and laughter. Wine flowed freely while Ovid spoke poetically of changing things. I confess that last night I seemed to understand his words completely, but today their meaning is as evasive as my husband Tiberius who is once again in self-imposed exile. I will have to pay the price for my wandering ways. I speculate on the punishment soon to come and just how long this house arrest will be. I am convinced it will be lengthy. We definitely should not have gone to the public fountain. Fannius, Varro, Thallus and I were the foolish ones who stayed until the early hours of the morning. Phoebe had no choice but to wait until I was ready to go home. Ovid and Berenice went home at a decent hour, as was their usual practice.

I arrange the folds of my tunic modestly as if it might conceal some of the mistakes from last night. Only a few hours ago, I arranged it to reveal the outline of my ample bosom. But, today, I shall be the epitome of reserve. To fasten the tunic, I choose the cameo brooch that features the sharp geometrical profile of my step-mother Livia. The brooch has a life of its own and speaks of Livia's wisdom: "First of all the festivities bring good times, then good times along with problems, and finally, just the problems." I now understand her advice.

"Well, open the gates to Hades, if she is not right again!" I cast the brooch a haughty look.

I will beg forgiveness, on bended knee if it comes to that. Once again, I muse, I have made a huge error in judgment. I shake my head from side to side at my own stupidity. But, this time, I feel strongly that I am ready to change my life, wasting no more days in the hazy zone of a blue grey fog. I am thirty-seven years old now. The time is right. I nod my head in agreement. These wrinkles are really becoming deeply entrenched, and furthermore, I do not have any desire to become slack-jawed. Tiberius and I enjoyed pointing out to each other the senators whose mouths would purse like little birds waiting to be fed and watered at sundown in expectation of things to come. I do not wish to become the brunt of my own joke. "Yes, my apology will be a most sincere one." I speak the words aloud and am somewhat reassured by my own resolve.

Indeed, if I am to succeed with my ultimate plan of winning back my father's favour, I will have to bow to Livia and her darling son, Tiberius. I shall become the model wife, the epitome of grace and virtue, and I shall not think unkindly towards Tiberius. I shall hold him in high regard as a good wife ought to do. I wince at the incongruity of it all. "Well, I could at least try harder," I sigh with the effort it will take. Tiberius was difficult enough as a brother. Our new relationship as husband and wife is simply too confusing to grasp.

I did not get a chance to thank Damaris for making me somewhat presentable. I make a mental note to thank her later. I suppose she is in a hurry to give her report to Livia. "That is to be expected," I sigh once again.

Snatching a mint leaf, I chew with grim determination in hopes that this will help my jumbled mind think more clearly. Just then the escort arrives. I walk ahead of the guards trying to muster a posture of dignity. Mesmerized by the rhythm of their disciplined footsteps, I fall into step. The corridor leading to the judgment hall seems to extend itself unrealistically, making me feel like a captive of time. I notice a small bit of dust left behind by the usually diligent cleaners. The white walls are awash with morning light. A gecko hides in the corner. Breaking out in a cold sweat, I instinctively rub my clammy hands on my tunic leaving an oily stain. I manipulate the folds of my tunic into an unsatisfactory configuration in an attempt to hide the tell-tale signs of my anxiety. My mind commands me to run for my life, but my body stands frozen and refuses to obey. The guards nudge me forward. Their melismatic footsteps carry me to the meeting with the briskness and efficiency of the emperor they serve.

Standing very still, I look upwards to the great and mighty figure of Caesar Augustus. As if blinded by his glory, I shield my eyes. "This is my father," I say to reassure myself and find myself nodding as if in affirmation. I know not to speak first. I know my place. Taking a deep breath, I release it audibly, swallow hard. My heartbeat is out of rhythm. I am made aware of these bodily functions that are usually taken for granted.

Feeling very small in this vast room, I stand alone while my father glares at me. The silence is purposeful and prolonged. Focusing on his judgment throne, I try to distract myself from his stony gaze. With an iron grip of authority, he clutches the sceptre in his left hand. I see the curule chair he sits on in vivid detail. Its curved arms rise to the cap of an elaborately carved eagle's head, which is embedded with topaz eyes reflecting the bird's all-knowing wisdom. The eagle scans me methodically, first with one eye and then the other, taking its time contemplating my future while assessing my past. The mighty bird clenches the feather from a white dove, the symbol of the *Pax Romana*. The eagle's wing-span forms a protective arbour for the one seated below. The golden bird diminishes my father's size. More importantly, I can see all too well that in his mind's eye he feels as mighty and insightful as the eagle itself.

I quickly avert my eyes from Caesar Augustus' elevated footwear. "Composure," I silently chant the word over and over to myself. Involuntarily, the workings of my body are once more demanding attention. My palpitating heart rages so violently against my chest, I am certain the people can hear it. My legs wobble. I am becoming quite dizzy and disoriented. Determined not to pass out, I take deep, slow even breaths. My clammy hands, now sweating profusely, betray my anxiety. I look down at them contemptuously for exposing my fears.

With deeply furrowed brow, Augustus eyes me with a look of scorn. I cower. The cohorts of last evening's festivities are sitting in the front row like a murder of crows perched on a branch. It takes me a moment to recall which one of them was last night's paramour, convincing me all the more that it is time to change my ways. I quickly avert my eyes from Fannius and Varro. They do not dare to look up. Ovid and Berenice are dressed impeccably, looking incapable of sin. Thallus is positioned behind Augustus. Not one of them graces me with eye contact.

The charges against me are read by the court recorder. Facing me directly, he reads from his scroll: "Giulia, daughter of Caesar Augustus and Scribonia, you have been charged with corruption of the public morality. You have been charged with breach of loyalty to the Roman Empire. You have been charged with the oppression and corruption of a servant." I bristle at this charge and wonder just how much of last night's revelry my servant revealed. Probably, more than I remember, I think to myself. I cannot really blame Phoebe. It is her duty to answer to Livia or the powers that be. The recorder continues,

"And finally, you have been petitioned to be divorced from Tiberius." Well, not all bad, I surmise. I notice Tiberius' absence and secretly hope he will stay forever on the island of Rhodes in his self-imposed exile.

Caesar Augustus addresses the senate and the people of the court. He clears his throat and begins to read from his written text. "Corrupting the public moral," he shakes his head slowly from side to side as if in incredulous sorrow. He speaks in a reserved and controlled manner as he continues, "You bring shame to yourself, to this household and to the ideals of the *Pax Romana*. Do you think that one person's actions do not affect the action and thinking of others? Do you recognize your moral obligation to the people of Rome to be a model of dignity and modesty befitting your position? Do you not understand the shame and concern your actions bring to our entire family?" I lower my eyes to hide my shame. Caesar Augustus continues, "We must set the example first of all at home. The people look up to us for guidance. We are their role models. If the *Pax Romana* is to be successful, this early example of virtue, peace and high morals is imperative. We must work together to meet our goals." 'We' is a good sign, I reflect.

"Giulia," his voice rises like hot wax as he addresses me. "You have been encouraged to be a part of this progressive movement, to contribute to the transformation which will lead the Roman Empire into a better way of life. Our determination is strong, our resolve impenetrable. And what stands in our way, I ask?" My father answers his own question and bellows, "My own daughter. My own daughter!" he repeats. Then he loses control, not reading from his prepared script, as is his tendency. "How idiotic, absolutely idiotic!" he hammers the arms of his chair with his fist. His voice rising once again, he spews, "You crack-brained harlot, what were you thinking?" Closing his eyes he takes a moment to regain his composure. In the midst of the stony silence that follows, I dare to look up, striving for contact with anyone, but no one looks my way. All eyes are downcast as if this might help to make those involved invisible. As I look at my father, I notice his lips are pursed tightly together in the same gesture of shame and humiliation as my own. We share features such as hair colour and fair skin. This is reassuring, but not so reassuring is the tired look on his face, most certainly caused by my recklessness. Then I notice his wrinkled forehead. The deep furrow of his brow and his set jaw are familiar signs of his conviction.

Augustus breaks his angry tone and continues wearily, reading once again from his script. "Giulia, you have everything a person could want or need and in abundance. You have had the finest of husbands. How, I ask, could we have found a more suitable match than that of Tiberius? He is not deserving of such ingratitude or disloyalty." I think I detect a note of insincerity in my father's voice.

Oh yes, I think, let me give thanks for Tiberius, the lecherous reprobate. I close my eyes so as not to reveal such un-wifely thoughts. How quickly my resolution to be a better wife is broken.

Augustus focuses on the task at hand and reads on, his beady eyes resembles more and more those of an eagle. "You must suffer the consequences of your actions, Giulia. Instead of spinning wool or linen like a virtuous wife ought to do, you spin destruction. You are a weaver of evil." I purse my lips and lower my head to stifle an involuntary smile at my father's choice of words. He continues, "You are disloyal and a disgraceful. Your behaviour has been excused, not once or twice, but too many times to count. But does our compassion wear off on you? No, faster than you can boil asparagus, there you are making mischief again and dishonouring our household. You seem to have no shame, no dignity. You are no better than a common whore." A long pause of thoughtful conjecture on Augustus' part and discomfort on mine follows. I barely dare to breathe. Silence ensues, with not even a nervous cough from the spectators.

On the 5th day of March in the year 2 B.C. Caesar Augustus has decreed that Tiberius be granted a divorce from me, Giulia, on the grounds of adulterous behaviour, as substantiated by witnesses. Infidelity! I raise my own eyebrows and jerk my head back at the injustice of it all. First of all, I have a difficult time thinking of my step-brother as my husband. Secondly, his infidelity is obviously not to be taken into account. Last, and certainly not least, there is no mention of his abandonment, cruelty or abuse. I know the rules and chastise myself for erroneous thinking that my position entitles me to exemption like the rest of them. On the other hand, I see the injustice of it all. I succumb to my own thoughts, wanting to speak, but not daring to. Confusion mingles with remorse for my own stupidity and carelessness.

At the mention of 'March' I grasp a fleeting understanding of this morning's dream.

In a restrained manner, Augustus drones on about the virtues of the *Pax Romana* heralding in a time of peace and new possibilities. I am emotionally exhausted and only catch snippets of his words. My father drones on about fighting for peace. I silently muse on how one could fight for peace. On a different occasion I would have enjoyed pursuing this statement with my father. He has claimed that he values my opinions. Augustus continues on speaking about a simple and virtuous way of life, something I have heard so often lately that it ought to be committed to long term memory. Then he goes on about imperial blood ruling with their heads. A more devious response comes to mind. There is a fragment of something else about honouring slaves and servants, to which I take exception, as I am respectful in that regard. Of course, I am not in a position to vocalise my objections. Phoebe, my servant, is in many ways more of a friend than my cousin and friend, Berenice. I truly regret that I have dragged Phoebe into this sorry mess.

The serious tone of Caesar Augustus' voice commands me to leave these thoughts behind and refocus, which moment by moment is becoming increasingly difficult. A wave of fatigue overcomes me. I fear that I will not be able to stand much longer. I catch the end of his words: "You are set on a single-minded destructive course. Your wanton love of spirits and licentious behaviour is affecting us all. Now, I must protect our household and the Roman people before you destroy our credibility as a peace-loving virtuous family." I watch his tongue flit in and out like that of a viper and know this to be a sign of his ill temper. White-lipped now, he continues. "By the might of the Roman Empire, people have been saved and given a better life. Indeed, we have the power and resources to save all mankind, and yet we are not capable of saving one of our own. I must defend our honour and anything that threatens the good of the empire. I cannot deny my obligation and ignore this distasteful task any longer."

Caesar Augustus turns his face towards me and in a monotonous detached tone states: "Giulia, after considering the written accounts of the charges before me and after listening to the accounts of the witnesses, I find you guilty of corrupting the public moral. I find you guilty of breach of loyalty to the Roman Empire. I find you guilty of the oppression and corruption of a servant."

Caesar Augustus faces the senate and those with voting powers and asks for an agreement on his decision. They unanimously concur.

"Giulia, you are exiled to the island of Pandateria for five years, where you will live a simple life and perhaps acquire some of the virtues befitting a modest woman. There will be no wine and no men.

"Do you have anything to say for yourself?" Caesar Augustus asks.

"I will miss the wine," I reply in stony resolve.

II

Staggering, I grasp the courtyard wall with the painted scene of the masked performers, in a clumsy attempt to steady myself. The laughing faces blatantly taunt me. Feeling faint, I squat down placing my head between my knees until the room stops swirling. Beads of perspiration form on my forehead. I stare at the masked actors. Their tears of laughter drip red iron oxide and brown sepia, mirroring my own stained face. I do not want to be a part in their cruel play. Contrarily, I stretch out my arms pleading for their help. My pathetic pleas distress me further. The masked figures with their vacuous eyes pay me no heed. I cover my ears to block out their mockery.

I push myself upright and stumble back to the safety of my room. Just in time, I dry heave into the basin. Misery and self-pity mingle with thoughts of lovers, friends, family, and gods who have all forsaken me.

I collapse on my bed and fall into a fitful sleep. My dream is vivid:

> *I am one with the eagle in its graceful beauty, swooping and gliding, my wingspan stretched to a great expanse, veering to the right and then to the left in a sensuous flight that evokes a sense of wild freedom. Abruptly, the eagle turns on me. Its talons are sharp as an arrow. Piercing yellow eyes, filled with menace, jolt me into consciousness.*

I awaken, panic stricken, gasping for breath.

Shaking off the grogginess, I try to make some sense of the dream. It speaks of the freedom I take for granted that will soon be gone. Although I feel so confined by the duties that bore me, like weaving, decorating, accounting, and managing a household, I would give anything to have these taxing matters back. The rules are just as confining. Whom I might see and whom I might not see is not a choice granted to me. As a matter of fact, whom I might marry was also not a choice granted to me. Still I have lots of company, and I am adept in getting around the rules and duties. I do not mind practicing script. Even though I am expected to model Livia's handwriting, I insist on keeping my own distinctive hand. All these things are meant to keep us women from being idle.

This is never a concern for me, for I can always find something interesting to do like gambling or shopping or secret liaisons. Yes, freedom to make choices, even poor ones, is a privilege that the dream portends will soon be gone.

The dream is a brief respite from the pessimism invading my mind like a plague that will not give up until it takes its toll of sacrifices. Blood rushes to my head as I recall Berenice feeding Tiberius a fig, his mouth pursed open expectantly like a baby bird. It gives me grief and heartache to realize that my friend would trade our lifelong relationship for a chance to win his favour. Episodes like this and many others with both Tiberius and Berenice, give me cause to withdraw from people and their confusing mannerisms. Berenice's habit of eye-rolling at others' inadequacies troubles me. I fear I might be found guilty through association. I suspect I am also subject to this gesture of contempt. Now that I am conveniently out of the way, Berenice might get what she wishes for. I would not want this for my friend's sake, since Tiberius can be very morose, stubborn and vindictive. The truth is I miss my friend already, and I have not even departed. I wonder why she has not come to see me. Perhaps she is not allowed to. I muse on the contradictory feelings I have for my friend. Morbid thoughts are rampant today, flitting like the honey bee from flower to flower.

Next, my rambling mind turns to the time I was shocked by the announcement of my impending marriage to Tiberius, whom I considered to be a brother. I confess, I did not think he was worthy enough, even sending a note to my father stating my concerns. Then thoughts turn to the death of my young husband Marcellus at only 19 years old, then the death of my next husband Agrippa, and then the stillborn child Tiberius and I were eagerly anticipating. We named him Aquila, bless his tiny little soul. And soon, I shall have to face the separation from my children. Next it seems like every injustice ever committed against me comes rushing to my mind. I worry that I might go mad, squeezing my head between my hands as if to keep me intact. I cringe as I recall the anger coming from my father's fists as he thumped the arm of his curule chair. As my life's dreams evaporate, a shroud of utter despair engulfs me. I fall back to sleep muttering apologies to indifferent walls for my own failures and poor choices.

It seems as if all the grief flowing through the household is filling the pore spaces with darkness.

I remind myself that in just three more short weeks I will be banished. I can hardly believe in the reality of this.

I write my father a letter of appeal. The letter looks simple, but it is an ominous task. I struggle with words, choosing, omitting, discarding then reinserting. I mull over the style: direct, indirect, pleading or piteously begging. Shall I be crisp and forthright? Shall I tell him that I shall perish without his good company? Even though this is the truth it does not sound authentic. With too many doubts and questions, I almost wear the wax out from melting and smoothing. In the end I write it in my own hand on papyrus with my best hand-writing.

Signed in my own hand without wax, Giulia daughter of Caesar Augustus.

To my father, I send greetings.

I have brought sorrow and shame upon our household, for which I am truly sorry. I am writing you out of grief and distress as this tear stained papyrus will attest.

I cover my face with shame as I confront the wrongs I have committed. I accept full responsibility for my erroneous choices. I see all too clearly my childish need for affection and attention and my shameful ways of achieving this.

I humbly beg you to forgive me once again knowing that I am not worthy of such a charitable act. I beseech you to help me to fully understand the edicts of the Pax Romana. With my hand placed over my heart, I pledge my allegiance to you, to the people of Rome and to the betterment of our society. As Romulus and Remus, our founders, are my witnesses I swear to this oath.

Finally, dearest father, please listen to this heartfelt appeal. Begging you on bended knee, I plead for forgiveness and promise to bring honour to our household.

May peace be with you.

Upon signing off, I recall my mother Scribonia telling me that she overheard conversations on the streets of the people making pleas for my return to favour. She also said that they told her that my presence enlivened the spirit of the place. My thoughts turn to the people. I realize that the plebeians know what it is to suffer adversity, but I also know they will have to stifle their pleas so as not to jeopardize their own welfare. I hope they do not forget me and will remember me for things other than an open purse. I worry about the future of the sick children, as their vulnerability touches my heart. I have asked Scribonia if she might carry on with this charity, so in need are they of supplies, medicine and a kind word. She complained she was too old, but in the end has made a vow to do so. I do not dare ask her to open her purse to the beggars, for she avoids them out of fear of disease, recoiling at their uncleanliness and inflictions. It would be unfair of me to ask Berenice. The begging bowl is a reminder that we must accept the things that are offered freely.

It is a sad thing to realize that making choices will no longer be a privilege afforded to me. What I might give and what I might not give will no longer be an issue. Where I choose to shop or how my hair ought to be dressed will no longer be an ordinary part of my day. I will have no place to go and no one to look appealing for.

As I look into the mirror, I see a reflection of my deteriorating condition and ask myself if I really care. My usual roberant complexion is now putrid yellow and blends in with the polished brass, almost causing my image to disappear. The only rebellion I have left in me comes from my body, made evident by loosened stools, numbness, aches and pains and this unrelenting fever. I try to convince myself that I will be just fine, even though I am fast losing faith in family, friends, myself and especially Livia's favoured god, Isis, whom she coaxes me to worship. Maybe I will not be fine. Maybe I will not be strong enough.

Damaris shuffles into my room and announces that she will be accompanying me into exile. I am quite surprised by this and wonder why Livia's servant is assigned to this task.

"What about Phoebe?" I inquire. "She will be joining us also, I assume." I am disappointed that Phoebe has not been with me these past few days and a little irritated by the inconvenience of having to deal with a different servant. I suppose it is Livia's idea, needing to scrutinize my every move. I miss Phoebe, as she is also a faithful companion.

The comb falls from Damaris' hand clattering to the floor. Damaris trembles visibly and stammers, "Do not you know?"

"Know what?" I ask.

"She is dead." Damaris cries. "Dead…her own hand," she stammers. Not caring about the appropriateness of such an action, she sits down, resting her head in her hands and succumbing to the grief of losing a dear friend.

Moments earlier, I could never have imagined that anything else might affect me. I thought I had reached my capacity for bad news. Feelings of shame overwhelm me as I question whether this might be my fault. I had used Phoebe as a scapegoat, to steal into the night on the pretext of going for a late night stroll. I led her to her own demise just as if I had floured and salted her myself. I lick my lips as if it might wash away the bitter taste of Phoebe's spent blood. I mutter, "This cannot be true." I desperately hope this is just another bad dream. This is one dream that I hope will evaporate quickly. I plead with Damaris to tell me this is just a bad dream. "Is it not?" I blubber.

Damaris cannot, will not console me.

My servant and Damaris' friend Phoebe, a gentle woman, now lies dead, an innocent victim of my pranks and follies. Filled with remorse, I watch Damaris shuffle out of the room. Her silence is palpable. What could she possibly say? How could she possibly answer my questions? I cannot blame her.

Left to myself, I recall the words of my father in regards to Phoebe and remember something being said about being as honourable as Phoebe. "Surely he did not think it would be honourable for me to kill myself," I mumble. "Surely he did not think that." With knitted brow I try to recall as much as possible. Then I remember being confused over the charge of corrupting a servant. These bits and pieces do not make any sense.

"Oh no, what have I done? Phoebe. How could you?" I ramble on. "You did not do anything wrong. You were only there because I requested that you accompany me."

I feel a heavy weight on my shoulders. This shall be my cross to bear.

* * * * * * * * * * *

The next few weeks are spent in preparation for exile. I am too confused and despondent to care about belongings. I leave most of the details up to

Damaris and Scribonia. Scribonia, who is usually harsh and prone to emotional outbursts, is uncharacteristically silent, intent on choosing the essentials and taking great care with each decision. I am grateful. My mother's shrill voice makes her countenance disagreeable even if it is not intended that way.

There had been some discussion as to whether or not Scribonia would join me in exile, but in the end it was decided that she should stay in Rome and visit periodically. I think I am relieved, but I am not sure of anything these days.

My mother resides in the women's court at the rear of an apartment complex, well removed from the home of Livia and Augustus. It is a place for the widowed, divorced and wizened. Some of the apartments are used as classrooms for training girls and women how to be virtuous and industrious homemakers, how to work wool and spin and sew, learn the nuances of proper etiquette and, among other things, to manage an allowance. I am always uncomfortable there, slow to learn and impatient. The gossip is usually interesting and helps to while away the time, but I am always happy to leave. I shudder to think that this might be my home when I return from exile, now that I am divorced from Tiberius and not a likely candidate for a new match that would bring power and prestige to the empire. I suppose I should have thought about these things earlier. It is futile to think of such things now. I shake my head hoping to dismiss these thoughts.

Reaching my capacity for sorrow and emotional trauma, I try to will my heart to harden against family and friends who have abandoned me. I resolve to walk with some semblance of dignity, although it is difficult to straighten my shoulders, so heavily laden are they. My muscles are taut with pain. I walk like 'bent over woman', a name Berenice and I had given to the woman who sold wool at the market. We speculated that her stooped posture was from too many hours toiling over her spindle. Now I wonder if she did not have an unbearable sadness. "Who knows?" I ask no one in particular.

The time has come to say goodbye to my five beloved children. As each child comes to me little bits of stoic resolve fall away like kernels of wheat. All five were sired by my second husband Marcus Agrippa: Gaius, Lucius, Giulia the Younger, Agrippina and Agrippa, born posthumous.

Gaius and Lucius arrive wearing their togas of manhood.

At a very young age they had been adopted by my father, who paid for them by symbolically striking a penny three times on a scale. Gaius and Lucius are favoured by their grandfather and when dining sit with him on the lowest couch, which is a place of honour. When Augustus makes a journey with the two boys they either ride by his side or, if my father is on horseback, precede him in a carriage. They are raised in Augustus' own household with the best of teachers and even encouraged to take on Augustus' handwriting as a model for their own. I am very proud of my sons and their relationship with my father.

I hug Gaius and Lucius and pat their backs, not wanting to release them. I hope to commit into long term memory the feel of their bodies and the sensation of their beating hearts. Feeling their discomfort, I immediately release them. Their watery unmanly eyes avoid my gaze. I gently push them away with these parting words: "my dearest sons, I am so very proud of both of you."

Agrippa, the youngest, not yet 10 years old and still wearing the bordered toga for boys, enters to say his farewell. Agrippa was not adopted by my father but in keeping with the upbringing of young boys is raised and schooled in the men's quarters. Agrippa has a violent temper and is prone to outbursts. He stands before me kicking at the floor and refusing to make eye contact. Agrippa does not care to be touched. Without thinking, I give him a quick hug and a kiss on the forehead, which he immediately wipes away with his hand.

"Be brave, my dear little boy," I tell him. My heart goes out to this poor little fellow that only a mother could manage to love. I lower my eyes, as a twinge of doubt casts a shadow over my ability to understand agape love.

I barely hear his reply, "mama," which is more of a whimper. I let out a huge sigh and squeeze back tears as if begging them to stay in check. Scribonia is waiting at the door to take away her kicking and screaming little grandson.

I have a fierce headache now that only the gallows might release. I feel like there is not a speck of light left in my world. My daughter, Giulia the Younger, enters the room. Her frail little body gives the false impression that she is still a child, although she is 17 and already married with a child of her own. Giulia the Younger is prone to anxiety attacks, worrying incessantly about everything and anything. She is socially inept, always saying or doing the wrong thing at the wrong time. I can manage to placate her in times of great stress by combing her hair. Remembering this, I stroke my daughter's hair tenderly and hold her close to my breast like a mother hen gathering her chicks under her wings. I hold her for a long time and then release her with our special secret kiss. I kiss her first on one cheek and then she kisses me on my cheek. It is important that our kiss be reciprocal. We gulp back sobs with a response that leaves us both limp as a foxglove that has become too heavy to bear its own weight.

I draw in a deep breath and release it as my youngest daughter, only 12 years old enters the room.

Compared to her older sister, Agrippina is by far the more mature. She is confident, quiet and intelligent. I will not have to worry about Agrippina. Besides, Livia has taken a liking to her and treats her like her own daughter. As long as their relationship remains favourable I will not have to concern myself with her welfare. Agrippina is more reserved in her affection than the other children, which at this point is a blessed relief. Agrippina grips my shoulders and squeezes them firmly. She hugs me, giving me the strength I need. I feel inadequate trying to impart on my brave daughter the deep feelings I have for her. Words elude me, so I just squeeze my daughter back.

A sense of numbness overwhelms me as the last of my children leave. I want so much to impart on them a love and a sense of security that will have to last them for five long years. I also want to warn them to keep their backs to the wall.

Scribonia enters the room chastising me for putting them all through this ordeal. The trill of her voice is not specific to this occasion. It is a constant source of embarrassment to me. My father tells me it was her bad character that was the cause of their divorce. I suspect that the crestfallen look on my face must have caused my mother to reconsider, since she stopped speaking in mid-sentence. Scribonia purses her lips tightly, willing herself to stop the flow of words. The two of us fall into each other's arms, weeping until all our tears lose their saltiness.

Beware the ides of March
(Shakespeare, "Julius Caesar")

III

The gods refuse to intervene, despite all my creative pleas. My destiny seems to be stamped out, not just with the Imperial seal, but apparently with the god's seal of approval for a good riddance. Neptune cooperates fully and deems that the sea passage will open for the season. Damaris, Dilf, Mishma and I will soon be on our way destined for the small island of Pandateria.

Pandateria is a place of exile for troublesome women of the Empire, or a place of retreat for members of the Imperial family, particularly in the summer months when Rome becomes stifling hot. Pandateria is a small elongated island, only three kilometres by one kilometre, located twenty-five nautical miles off the coast of Italy in the Tyrrhenian Sea. The island was formed by an ancient volcano, with a natural cliff surrounding the villa. This makes it a strategic haven or an inescapable prison, depending on one's circumstance. My father withdraws to this island or to the Island of Capri for rest and rejuvenation whenever he can manage.

Surrounded by a deep turquoise blue sea, Pandateria might be considered by some to be an earthly paradise. But for me, this isolated place will be a living hell.

The journey this time of the year will be uncomfortable. March at the best of times has an unpredictable nature. Today is cold and dismal, a testament to March's mood, which swings like the scales of justice from sunny and bright one day to damp and dreary the next. I suppose comfort is not high on my father's priority list, whereas expediency is. Augustus seems rather determined to go through with this.

It seems Tiberius, my father and I have more in common than we realize with our experience of exile. Tiberius has spent the better part of past four years on the island of Rhodes, claiming he needs respite from public affairs even though he is young and healthy and in his prime. I suppose he is escaping our unhappy marriage. Tiberius has become increasingly apprehensive about his grooming for leadership and consequently has grown more spiteful towards me, blaming me for the acceleration of his duties. He seems to be more fearful for his life as a result of his newfound status. He has become quite curt with his mother, even avoiding her. According to my dear husband, his former life was just as he liked it. Before our marriage, he was happily married to Vipsania, looking forward to the birth of their child. I suppose he resents our marriage as much as I do. Tiberius blames me for all his miseries and failures. It seems to me that Vipsania's virtues grow with time. I do recall that she was a good wife, doting on him even when he was in one of his foul moods. I imagine that, like me, she was quite happy with his long absences. No one, not even Vipsania, would be immune to his foul moods. Unlike me, however, she managed to stay controlled. I know that I am too quick to retaliate. Unfortunately, I am aware of these things too late. I made the mistake of thinking myself free from the confines of marriage during his absences. Come to think of it, I made lots of mistakes.

Then there is my father confining himself to his suite, quite likely until I am out of sight. As for me, unlike my father and my husband, I shall not take to exile, so willingly. This much I know. Most of the time, I like to be with people, preferring to have the choice to withdraw from them whenever they tax my patience.

Scribonia shares the gossip about Tiberius with me. She says that the people deem him to be a queer sort with his self-imposed exile and his willing abandonment of his family and duties. His reticence about his new status perplex the multitudes, since many would be more than pleased to trade places with him and acquire his privileged lifestyle. They say that if it were not for his mother's status, he never would have reached such lofty heights. Rumours of his deviant behaviour are also a topic of whispered conversation. As rumours go, I suspect they are ambivalent, sometimes exaggerated or sometimes underestimated. His popularity, what little there ever was, is waning like the winter months. Speculation has it that our arranged marriage was the catalyst that triggered his peculiar behaviour and his increasing lust for virgins and young boys. I can attest that this was not the trigger and that his perverse acts of sexual deviance and cruelty are nothing new. I have bite marks to prove this. I recall one particular night, early in our marriage, when Tiberius brought a virgin to our bedside. Blindfolding her, he slapped her and cracked a whip to terrify her further. Not until she was weeping bitterly was he satisfied. When he took the blindfold off, he innocently looked towards me and asked, "Why did you strike her?" I was as much a pawn in his sexual exploits as the young woman. Afterwards, Tiberius left the room dismissing me with a look of contempt and words that implied that I was not loving enough and therefore responsible for his lagging libido.

I dismissed the young woman with a harshness that she likely did not deserve. At the time, I felt no remorse, only anger for her presence and her youthful body.

I blame our marriage for a shift in my behaviour. I see now, all too clearly, how I sought attention and developed a taste for wine, which seemed to help my flagging sense of esteem. It shames me to think how I resorted to this naïve behaviour.

Also, our relationship was to change dramatically from brother and sister to man and wife. Because we share the same parents, we shared a good part of our childhood. In spite of common experiences, we developed different attitudes in regards to leadership. Tiberius is unlike his mother, who has a genuine zest for power. He does not have that same zeal for prestige and for ruling the Empire. As for me, my childhood fantasy of ruling by my father's side was delusional. Ruling by Tiberius' side would be simply humiliating and demeaning, much like our love life.

It is no wonder that with all these changes Tiberius also became confused and contradictory. As time moves on, he abuses his power, becoming crueler and more demanding. When my father ordered him to return to Rome he threatened to starve himself. I was coerced by Livia into writing Tiberius a letter pleading with him to save himself. My father's reply to Tiberius' refusal was "oh, never to have married and childless to have died." I really resented being included in this reprimand, but I did not voice my concerns. My father sent out an edict that Tiberius must in the future request permission to return to Rome. I am pleased to say that when Tiberius did make the request, it was denied. Livia pleaded on his behalf to have Tiberius named a legate of Augustus in order to stave off Tiberius' humiliating failure to accept his role in life. I assume her pleas were also to placate her own admission of failure in regards to our marriage, which was meant to strengthen the Empire not diminish it.

Livia's ambitious plans have gone astray. Her grave disappointment in us is evident in her demeanor towards me. According to her, Tiberius, her beloved son, has so much promise. She proclaims him to be a gifted orator and repeatedly sites Tiberius' speech, when he was only twelve years of age, at his father's funeral. If it is up to her, people will not forget. Truly, the speech was admirable. She touts his role as an accomplished equestrian and proudly shows off the statue of him and his horse at every opportunity. Livia reminds my father that Tiberius is also an adept organizer, planning gladiatorial games and races with appropriate fanfare. He is diplomatic, giving honour or paying homage to others when it is due them. Livia must wonder how all this promise went so wrong.

Tiberius was made legate. I ought not to ignore Livia's persuasive powers over my father.

I received a letter from Tiberius informing me he was quite right to divorce me, given the circumstances. You would think the idea was his own and not on Augustus' authority. Besides, Tiberius added, my impertinence would surely lead the other women of the Empire astray. He generously said that I am to keep all the things he gifted me with. He wrote a letter to Augustus requesting the same. He also requested I receive a fair allowance, which he has offered to administer.

According to Scribonia, he had asked permission to attend my trial. Permission was denied. Knowing Tiberius as I do, this will only make him more suspicious of the motives of others. I know through Tiberius' actions and words that he is becoming distrustful of the growing allegiance between my sons Gaius and Lucius and my father Caesar Augustus. This is evident through his incessant questions. He began treating visitors with suspicion and eventually testing his most trusted allies to see if they were involved in a rebellion against him.

I suspect he will be vacillating between withdrawing from the Roman world and conniving to return to his position as a valuable ally to my father. He will have to depend on his mother to look after his best interest and return him to favour. Quite likely, she will do a splendid job.

* * * * * * * * * * *

Damaris – whose name means heifer

While I sit waiting in the litter, I am filled with pity at the sight of Giulia standing alone. A sharp morning shadow casts her outline on the pavement. I will her to move and come and sit beside me. My will is not strong enough. She does not respond.

Even though it is apparent the people are here to support her, Giulia appears diminished.

I am not sorry to leave Rome. My friend Cornelius is the only person I shall miss. I look back to check on Dilf and Mishma. They are also immobilized. We wait.

Looking up, I see Augustus' and Livia's quarters situated on the Palantine Hill, one of the seven hills on which Rome was built. The colonnaded palace overlooks the Circus Maximus, where they can view a good portion of the track for the chariot races. Augustus' own modest house is sparsely furnished, with unadorned tile floors and walls with no murals, in keeping with his own fondness for austere settings and simplicity. Livia's house is more decorative, giving preference to fine furnishings, expensive works of art and fine weavings that reflects her good taste. They share a courtyard, with hanging bougainvillea supported by a lattice wall, providing them with a semblance of privacy.

This courtyard is where Cornelius and I met for discussions. The demands of Livia and Augustus left us with little time for exchanging news. The past while, with so much happening, we could barely wait to see each other.

Only yesterday, Cornelius told me Augustus is too ashamed to leave his quarters. Cornelius had spoken to Augustus about the pleas of mercy for Giulia from the general population. Cornelius and I shared these sentiments. He felt it prudent to plead through a third party, given Augustus' present state of turmoil. More openly, Cornelius spoke of Giulia's generosity and kindness, reminding Augustus also of her spirited personality which often delighted him.

"We will miss her, just as I am sure you might," Cornelius confided with me that he had expressed these words cautiously when addressing Augustus.

"Why do not you ask me if I will miss this festering boil on my neck?" Augustus had bellowed back to him. "We will speak no more of this," he answered Cornelius with a tone that demanded allegiance.

Cornelius thought it was evident Augustus was humiliated by his daughter's promiscuous and rebellious behaviour. The sudden disappearance of Antonius did not produce the desired results of Giulia's loyalty towards Tiberius. Augustus was also suspicious of Antonius' loyalty to himself. There would always be others willing to take Antonius' place. Although Cornelius is Augustus' confidante, he kept this part to himself. Augustus dismissed Cornelius with orders for no more discussions on the matter. Augustus withdrew into the solitary confinement of his house until the exiles departed and he regained some sense of composure. No one interfered with his request for solitude, not even his doting wife Livia.

I reflect on recent conversations with Cornelius. It was evident Augustus was in a hurry to rid the household of any visible reminder of his failure to control his children. As head of the household and as a ruler whose greatest virtue is strength, Giulia's presence spoke eloquently of Augustus' mortal limits. Augustus remarked to Cornelius that even Livia has been exasperated with her failed attempts to refine Giulia's manner, and that if Livia could not succeed then indeed it was quite likely that no one could. Augustus longed for a respite himself and surmised that exile to his beloved island of Pandateria was not the punishment that his daughter's crime deserved. He likened his daughter Giulia and his grandchildren, Giulia the Younger, and Agrippa to the festering boils currently oozing puss and keeping him in a state of pain and vexation. The boils lie dormant waiting to erupt at the least provocation, just like his children who are constantly taxing his spirit and keeping him from the more important matters of state. Augustus' spirited dream of Rome as ruler of the world, heralding a new day of peace and well-being, would have to be postponed until his household returns to a state of equilibrium and the pain from his blistering sores subsides.

I was aghast that Augustus would speak of his children in such a spiteful manner, but I understood his exasperation. Cornelius and I sympathized with his lack of control over Giulia.

I can see Giulia from where I sit. She does not move. I suppose she is waiting and hoping that someone will come to her rescue.

Perched high above the gathering crowd on a balcony strategically built to overlook the city square, Livia stands stoically waving good-bye to Giulia. For her, this position is meant to convey the impression of a solid dependable presence in this time of adversity. However, she is wrong about the impression she conveys, for the people, including myself, recognize her disdain. In our eyes, Livia always manages to be distanced in some way, either guarded by a tangible wall or some intangible barrier of condescension. Knowing Livia as I do, if she had been aware of the negative impact she was conveying, it would be remedied. She is a perfectionist in dress as well as demeanour. Livia prides herself on being a woman of unshakeable conviction. She is an ambitious woman, constantly striving towards supreme reign and ensuring a continuation of lineage for her family as ruling members of the Roman Empire.

Cornelius and I agreed that the marriage between Tiberius and Giulia had not gone according to Livia's detailed plan. I thought this well-rehearsed plot resembled a theatre production gone wrong, with dejected actors scurrying off the set after a poor performance. Provisional rules would have to be enforced, since Livia forgot to consider that what goes on behind the curtain also matters.

For now, Livia stands stoically posed, one hand resting on her cheek in thoughtful conjecture and the other hand resting on the marble balustrade. She is the picture of refined taste, impeccably dressed in a simple finely woven tunic with a grey woolen cloak. As always, her hair is neatly dressed. With an appropriate look of foreboding, Livia scans the horizon with her eyes above the heads of 'her people'. In my view, her carefully staged presence is in vain for two reasons. First, the people tired long ago of even attempting reciprocal eye contact. Secondly, all eyes are focused on Giulia.

I think under different circumstances the people might revere Livia for her rock-solid demeanour and her refined taste. She is a visible example reinforcing the projection of strength and dignity that is attributed to the Roman Empire. "Strength mirrors strength", is one of her favourite mantras. Livia keeps a mental list of friends and foes, which she cunningly uses to her advantage.

Below Livia's perch, there is a queue of people lining up several rows deep as far as the eye can see. The people are here to pay their respects to Giulia and bid her farewell. The normal robust sounds of a waking city are subdued, as if in sympathy with the exiles. Many of them have suffered from adversity under the rigid and ambitious rules of the Empire. The majority sympathize with Giulia's plight. Giulia has kept their spirits high with her vibrant countenance. Phoebe attested to her generosity and compassion for the sick and outcasts. Phoebe told me Giulia's generosity came from the heart, which was made evident by impromptu actions, opening her purse to the afflicted and seldom bartering at the market.

My thoughts turn to the governing body of the Roman Empire. It has a posture of generosity when used to promote its own virtue and to instill a sense of worthiness in the common people. The iron hand of justice deals firmly and harshly with the people when necessary. Taxes are assessed and reassessed in order to pay for growth. The plebeians are told this is for the good of all. Roads and bridges, ports and arenas are raised along with the taxes. The deep pockets of the senators are lined with the hard work of the plebeians, who are either complacent with their own comfort or fearful of retribution if they complain too loudly. The citizens are not foiled by the contradictions and propaganda, but realize it is prudent to be cautious with criticism. The Roman hierarchy has a way of rewarding the people for patriotism, making even the conquered folks, like myself, feel like Roman citizens. The Empire instills a sense of strength and might in the people. They, in turn, accept and integrate this into their psyche with enthusiasm. I should like to share these thoughts with Cornelius. But today I will lose yet another friend. I will miss him dearly.

I smile as a memory flashes before me of Cornelius. The two of us share a conversation on the *Pax Romana*. I imagine his voice. "Now, in the favoured words of their ruler, Caesar Augustus, 'faster than you can boil asparagus', the people are supposed to change their thinking and become a peace-loving people." Cornelius said the *Pax Romana* has too many rules that are too restrictive. He respects the concerns of the Roman citizens for their vulnerability now that they are supposed to be a peace-keeping nation as opposed to the mighty conquerors of only yesterday. They are conditioned to speak with weapons and not with honey. These new habits will require an adjustment in thinking. For now, it is confusing and frightening, as change usually is.

As challenging as it was, Cornelius and I managed, quite nicely, to solve all the problems of the Roman Empire. We held each other's opinions in high regard. Our conversations had no boundaries and included topics such as politics, society, punishment, art, values, and all such important matters of the day. Respect is a good quality to have in a friend.

Cornelius and I often discussed Giulia's rebellious character. She was aware of the rules prohibiting her from associating with anyone other than those approved by Livia or Augustus. Caesar Augustus wrote a letter to Antonius to reproach him for visiting Giulia without consent. A few months ago, Giulia and Antonius were seen together at the forum, publicly displaying their affection for one another. Unfortunately for the two of them, their disregard for decorum was reported in the daily chronicle. Cornelius told me that Augustus was furious. He would not divulge what punishment Antonius received. I did not ask, as admittedly I do not desire to know.

We understand that Giulia is the sacrificial goat that is supposed to help the public realize the consequences of their actions if they do not accept this new vision of peace, order and high morals.

As is the case in most communities, the people are not all sympathetic in regards to Giulia's banishment. The harshest amongst them feel her punishment is too lenient, and consequently she deserves to be stoned. There are those who take macabre pleasure in her downfall, as it makes them feel more superior. There are those who delight in the opportunity to gossip. The banishment certainly provokes discussion. Augustus has been looked up to, frowned upon, vindicated, justified, ridiculed, and revered, all with caution and reservation, since it is not wise to be too vocal about the shortcomings of the ruling class. Basically, the people, even the conquered, are loyal to the Roman Empire. Rewards are part of their conditioning. Patriotism is instilled easily, as the people themselves become instantly allied with the strong and the powerful. Governing is a virtue of the Roman Empire, and they are good at it. Family dynamics are another matter entirely.

I shall miss Cornelius. I look up towards Augustus' balcony. I see Cornelius, vigorously waving a white cloth. I wave back, feebly, then with more enthusiasm. I want him to know that I see him.

Giulia turns. With a sigh heavily laden with reality, I climb out of the litter to await her arrival.

IV

Even though it is early morning and the air still cool, my forehead is soaked with perspiration. Ambling over to the statue of my father, I find relief in its shadow. Pressing my head against the coolness emanating from the statue, I raise my eyes to meet my father's gaze, which is as cold and hard as the marble itself. His skin is made smooth by the polished surface. The muscles and life-like veins bulge with youthful vigour. His all-knowing eagle eyes gaze unflinchingly towards the rising sun. The lyrical form of Caesar Augustus outlined against the sky projects an image of wisdom and authority. I cannot help but observe that there are no crooked little yellow teeth, too many for the jaw to hold, no thinning straw-like yellowing hair with bald spots, no rash, no furrowed brow or sagging skin. This statue is so life-like, yet so deceitful in its beauty. It is not real, I remind myself, but still I plead for intervention while clinging to a fracture of hope. I make my final appeal to my father's divine powers. Surely, his benevolent nature will return me to my rightful place, where I will be enfolded in forgiving arms and redeemed from my mortal sins.

As stoically as I can muster, I walk away from the ominous silence of the statue. I am aware of the deep flaws coursing through my own veins that I have so willingly revealed for all to see.

My father says that, like the spokes of a wheel lead to the hub, all roads will lead to Rome. "All but this one," I retort. The carriage that will carry us on the contrary road draws near. With stony resolve, I mount the temporary staircase to enter the curtained litter. Damaris follows with my traveler's bag.

I wave a feeble farewell to the people who have come to lend their support. Quietly, I speak parting words of farewell to those who have forsaken me. "Fine, then, to the everlasting fires of hell with the lot of you".

Dilf and Mishma will follow in another less comfortable litter. It is evident in their demeanor that they feel honoured to be in such a prestigious position as to be carried.

The slow rhythmic sounds of the carriers and the horses crunching along the gravel road are in concert with my grating nerves. I am having difficulty breathing. I know full well that this is caused by anxiety, but I place the blame on the dust that soon enough becomes a reality. The dust fills the pores of our skin and becomes embedded in the folds of our clothing. Conversation is impossible. We hold our scarves snuggly over our parched mouths.

After many milestone markers, earthly dry dust gives way to the freshness of salty air. The smell of mossy algae mingles with the fresh scent of cut lumber.

In the other litter, Mishma cocks his ear towards the sounds of the port with its birdsong, cats mewing, sea splashing and trees rustling. Keeping her scarf covered tightly to her nose, Dilf pretends that the dust still bothers her. As we all know, the putrid odour coming from Mishma lingers and cannot be masked in such close quarters.

A stirring comes from my bag. The look of horror in Damaris' eyes is almost laughable. I scoop out Livia's puppy, Moonbeam. The young pup burrows into my lap while nibbling my fingers. "Now, how did that little scalawag get here?" I query, with a look of dismay that only an accomplished actor could convey. This will likely be the only bit of sunshine we will experience this day. It gives me pleasure to recognize that I still have a modicum of impulsiveness. Of course, I am immediately regretful, as it is my impulsiveness that gets me into all kinds of trouble.

My eyes search the east for the forest that I am certain used to be here. I see that it has become a graveyard of felled trees, looking like beheaded sentinels. To the west, the newly built port is more expansive than anything imaginable. Wooden storehouses, docks, a stone lighthouse with arched portholes; everything is here for an efficient and monumental port. This is an engineering feat that only my father's vision could concoct. The smell of new construction is pleasing, holding fresh promises of growth and prosperity. Many large ships remain docked while being prepared for the upcoming season. The merchant ship we will travel in is a small vessel with two steering oars at the rear and eight on each side for the oarsmen. Damaris tells me it will take an hour or so for the provisions to be loaded, time enough for us exiles to stretch our legs.

To our delight, Moonbeam romps around, lifts her leg to urinate, and topples over in his excitement. He nibbles any toes that are foolishly exposed.

After boarding, the boatswain provides us with buckets. "Just in case the rise and swell of the sea is not in harmony with the fluid in your bellies," he proclaims. The boatswain's chapped and cracked lips form a devious grin that frames his decaying teeth, what few are left. He has the overall strange appearance and odour of being pickled. We exiles cannot help but notice his feet, which are gnarled and petrified like tree stumps buried beneath the forest floor. His toe nails are yellowed with deep ridges, sick with fungi. His legs are marked with strange striations reminiscent of wave-like patterns etched into the sand of the seashore. We attempt to divert our eyes from this sea creature but cannot help ourselves as we steal guilty glances.

All too soon, land is out of sight. The boatswain informs us that he is quite nervous about this part of the journey. He explains that a person can tell this is the deepest part of the sea because of the blackness of the waters. "There must be some good in this ill wind," he adds, "but if she decides to blow any harder, we will all be swallowed up by 'Old Jonah's whale'. And, we will not be the first ones, either." The wind has indeed picked up, and now our internal rhythms are rising and falling while the sea is falling and rising. Each of us, in turn, makes good use of our buckets.

After what seems like an eternity, the boatswain cries out, "Oh, by the gods of the sea. Look at the size of that whale!" He revels in the size of Dilf's eyes. Soon enough, we realize it is land rising out of the sea. Just across from the whale-shaped island, we catch sight of our destination.

Damaris' deep breath is heard by all of us. She has an odd expression that resembles happiness. I suppose she is just relieved to be safely on land.

Some of the islanders are waiting at the dock to help with the provisions. They are also here to greet us newcomers and to take delight in the green of our gills and our wobbly sea-legs. Their elbowing and snickering attest to this. I do not mind the jesting; it is the least of my concern.

It is early in the evening after a very long day. Our audible sighs reveal that we are all amazed and relieved that we are still amongst the living.

Damaris – whose name means heifer

V

As we exiles enter the sheltered port, the waves calm magically, as if the halcyon bird was awaiting our arrival. The exhausted rowers stretch their muscles for the last few strokes.

I see the harbour is a natural inlet enhanced with man-made piles providing protection from the unpredictable Tyrrhenian Sea. The pier is a familiar solid structure reminding me of the port we left hours ago. I feel gratitude for something firm beneath my feet. I breathe deeply, grateful to be alive. I glimpse natural caves, carved out by the sea, lining the port and serving as repair shops and storage houses. We exiles barely notice our surroundings or the people, so concerned are we with keeping our equilibrium.

Giulia, Mishma, Dilf and I are guided by the gatekeeper. We follow obediently on our wobbly sea legs. We make our way up the steep incline, zigzagging back and forth until we arrive at the summit, where the island plateaus. Not far from the port we reach a fork in the road. The gatekeeper explains that one path leads towards the town square and the other path towards the villa. He tells us that the entire island is only three kilometres long by one kilometre wide. Cornelius had told me that the villa is naturally garrisoned by steep craggy cliff walls making it an impenetrable fortress. Cornelius shared all this pertinent information with me in order to allay my misgivings. He spent many summers here with Caesar Augustus who needed respite from Rome's stifling heat.

The villa is not visible from this vantage point as the entry has high stone walls on both sides of the iron grilled gate, which is framed by a natural stone archway. The field stones and rocks lay horizontally, the mortar mingling with young moss. A vertical row of stones tops the wall. As Giulia followed by her servants, enter the villa grounds we hear a resounding clank as the lock of the gate slips into place. Immobilized, we stand still. Our minds attempt to grasp the reality of the moment.

Before us, an expansive garden presents itself with fountains and realistically portrayed garden nymphs frolicking in their watered prisons. The outdoor space has been planned meticulously with benches and covered alcoves strategically placed to benefit from either the sun or the shade, depending on one's preferred desires. The interior area is defined by columns with sloping roofs to collect rain water. Palm trees, agave plants, olive and lemon trees, and carved marble vases with reliefs of vegetation complete the area.

Beyond this flat expanse, a three-tiered staircase rises to the villa and its grounds. A columned archway with planters on each side leads to an atrium with the central part opening to the sky to let in light and to catch rain water for the central pool. This will help to keep the villa cool in the hot summer months. A statue of a dove appears to be snatching a sparkling jewel from a nest. A series of rooms on three sides, articulated by an open air colonnade with a pool in the middle along with the entranceway, completes the square plan. Access to all rooms is from the outside corridor.

I notice Caesar Augustus' penchant for simplicity in the sparsely furnished rooms of Giulia's suite. The bed room has a wardrobe for clothing, a large desk with a chair, and a high bed with a stool. There are two copper-clad windows the size of portholes. The sitting room holds two chairs and a table. A small room for the latrine and hot water bath is adjacent to her suite.

We make our way to the dining room. It is furnished with six reclining couches, which is actually five more than Giulia will need. A library with three desks and another bedroom complete the household rooms on the main floor. The library has three large frescoes on one wall. The first one is recognizable with a painting of Narcissus admiring his reflection in the still waters of the spring. I see Giulia shaking her head with what appears like pity at Narcissus self-absorption. Or is she mirroring herself? I suppose I have no way of knowing what her thoughts might hold. The other two do not capture Giulia's attention. Giulia mutters that there is not enough artwork to satisfy her taste. I notice that the dining room has beautifully carved vases and hope this will bring her some comfort.

I notice the tasteful but plain tableware stored on shelves along with a few ornaments. Some are familiar from Caesar Augustus' and Livia's travels. The cream coloured marble floor has no design or border, but it holds its own intrigue with natural golden coloured veins running throughout.

We proceed to the bathing rooms which face west to take advantage of the warm sun. In keeping with her father's love for bathing, there is a cold water bathing hall, adjoined by a warm water bathing hall and then a third room with a tub for hot water bathing. A latrine is positioned in the corner. The floor is inlaid with tiles of fish and marine life randomly set in cement. A marble border surrounds the scene from the sea. The upper part of the walls is adorned with scenes painted on plaster, consisting of a pod of frolicking dolphins on a Mediterranean blue background. The dolphins appear to swim from room to room. Dark blue glass mosaics shaped like waves border the bottom of the walls. Embedded veins, in the marble, mimic the water's movement. The faintest smile crosses Giulia's lips. I wonder if it is in appreciation of the artworks or if it is in recollections of her father's penchant for bathing.

All the other walls and tapestries in the villa are in harmonious shades of orange, gold and cream. The blue sky and the turquoise waters of the sea compliment the colours, giving it an ambiance of order and serenity.

The servant's quarters are situated in the upper rooms near the entrance to the villa and on the eastern side. Each room is equipped with a table, a lamp, a stool and a cot. It is adequate, I think to myself.

Above the main suite are two more upper rooms for lounging and sitting. These rooms open to a veranda providing an expansive view of the sea. The lower floor on the east side houses an amply stocked larder, which is adjacent to the well-equipped kitchen. I smile, and I know why. An outside wall defines the east corridor to keep the sounds from the kitchen from the rest of the villa.

An outdoor furnace serves as an oven for baking as well as supplying heat to the villa. Another fireplace below the bathing rooms supplies heat to the rooms and to the water tank. Plumbing and heating is state of the art, in keeping with Roman innovation. The villa is well equipped with latrines, a sewer system, ceramic water pipes, heating ducts and water pumps. Underground cisterns collect rainwater and channel the water to the villa. All these comforts will keep Mishma occupied.

Facing the west and outside the villa are several outdoor covered patios with large archways permitting a panoramic view of the surrounding sea. Giulia sees the layout of the villa and the grounds as resembling a ship. I see her observation, but I would have never noticed it on my own. At the prow, three descending brick terraces lead half way down to the sea with a sharp drop off overlooking the cliffs below. Neither one of us has the courage to go too close to the edge for fear of keeling over and tumbling to our death. As for myself, it is more a fear of drowning than being dashed against the rocks. The walls of the terraces are reinforced with intricate brick work angled diagonally to harmonize with the lay of the land. Looking forward, the starboard side facing east and the portside to the left and facing west are also surrounded by impenetrable cliffs. The entrance we recently passed through carries a stern reminder that this is the only way in or out. Giulia cuttingly remarks, "This is a perfect place for troublesome women of the empire".

Except for the locked gate, the comfort and serviceability of our home for the next five years seems to relieve Mishma and me of any concerns we might have. Dilf appears to be a little disconcerted. Giulia appears to be battle fatigued.

I gaze at Giulia, Mishma and Dilf and feel a heaviness deep inside.

VI

I am unappreciative of the meticulous space planned by my father for his optimum comfort and visual pleasure. When I wish to be alone, which is seldom a problem, I repair to my favourite spot on the cement steps leading down to the cistern. I need to get away from any reminder of the splendour of Rome. Even at my place of refuge, I am reminded of my father's passion for archways. There is even one over this staircase. One pillar is man-made, and the other support column consists of natural rock with a brick archway over the top. It is here that I can sit comfortably on the mossy step with my back nestled into the gentle curve of a large rock and be sheltered by the wind.

Today, as usual, I brood like a mother hen, obsessed with the safety of her chicks, over that fateful evening. It is here in this place that I can most clearly see my weaknesses, which are plentiful and seem to grow daily like the Black-eyed Susan that has magically sprouted a new vine overnight. I stare into the darkened eye of its deceitful, cheery yellowed face.

It is Phoebe's suicide that brings me the most pain and the most questions and the never ending unanswered pleas as to why.

"Better my own daughter," these words from my father's lips plague me with their intense scorn. The cold words sting like a March wind. As if in empathy, a spray from the ocean mingles with my own salty tears. Thinking about my own children, who had sometimes been a trial, one with his bad temper and another with her constant emotional outbursts, still, I cannot conceive of holding such bitter thoughts towards them. As for Phoebe, some days I am very cross with her for taking her own life, which gives me pause to reflect on my own callousness. How could I possibly be angry with her and how could I have such a peculiar reaction when she is not here to defend herself against this outrageous response?

If only I could turn back the time. I would not ask her to go with me. Consequently, she would still be alive, and then we would be busy preparing for some important social event. Life as I knew it would be routine again with all its interactions, gossiping, intrigue and entertainment. These familiar thoughts I live over and over, time and time again, always, expecting different results but never finding any solutions or making any progress, just like old Sisyphus trying to hang onto that damned rolling stone.

That fateful night, Thalus, usually serious in nature, was in an exceptionally jovial mood supplying us with plenty of un-watered wine and generously keeping our cups filled to overflowing. I do enjoy a cup or two of good wine, but this was obviously potent. Even though I was aware of this, I drank deeply and with the gusto of drunkard. That was my choice and a poor one, I must admit. The more wine I drink the wittier and wiser I become, completely understanding Ovid's poetry, when in more sobering times, often perplexes me. Last, but not least, I like how the wine makes me feel. It brings solace to my spirit, quelling anxieties and helping me to forget the unhappiness of my troubled relationship with Tiberius. Usually, I am more reserved in the amount I consume, simply because I enjoy life immensely and look forward to the endless possibilities a new day heralds, but regretfully not that night.

Our social life at the palace is rich. I mean to say that our social life in Rome is rich. My father despises it when I refer to our home as a palace. "I stand corrected," I speak the words to my absent father. There is always something to look forward to in Rome. Life is rich and full. Often, the preparations are as fulfilling as the event itself.

There is nothing enchanting about this place of banishment. There is nothing to stimulate the senses or challenge the mind. I cannot even fathom wanting to leave Rome to come here for a respite. Boredom and isolation leaves one ill willed and belligerent. Perhaps, this explains Tiberius' nasty disposition. I despise him. I despise this place. I despise what I have become, but I despise self-pity even more, so I shall overcome this moribund state. It will take more determination than I have at this moment.

I am rambling, I know, but my thoughts will not rest, not even for a moment.

That night, something was amiss. I cannot seem to pinpoint what it is that baffles me, nor can I recall any dead black birds, lightning or other such ill omens. Maybe there was an unfavourable wind that I missed, so preoccupied was I conniving with my cohorts over our secretive after dinner plans.

Livia's elaborate hair dressing stands out in the jumble of recollections. Two and a half hours was spent on my own dressed hair that was embellished with rose buds intricately entwined into braids and curls. None could compare to Livia's elaborate styling, which was most daring for her as she has a preference for fine quality and reserved dress. Livia makes an exception when it comes to precious jewels. Livia's face was framed with tiny curls. Nine braids were drawn together at the back of her head into a wreath resembling a seashell. Tiny curls formed at the centre, spiralling out into lustrous coils. I suppose part of it must have been a hairpiece, but one could not possibly figure out which was her own hair and which was not, so ingenious it was. To say the least, it was spectacular. You can wager that the women of the court will be copying it. But it will be too late, for it is always unforgettable to be the first in the latest fashion.

Unfortunately, I recall in vivid detail how my own hair looked, the morning after, with the wilted flower buds entwined with dry twigs. I suppose I did not care then, but I do now, seeing all too clearly the smudged eye make-up and the disheveled hair. Now, I am left with discouraging memories of withered hope, remorseful days gone by, and some burning questions. Why was the wine not watered? It is always prepared ahead of time and mixed in pitchers. What ill omens did I overlook? An event of this proportion would not happen without a warning. Why did Thalus join us? It is so out of character for him to join in the revelry. Was Phoebe's husband one of the guards? This might account for her humiliation if faced by her betrothed. Did he scorn her? Was she so ashamed that she would resort to such an extreme reaction? The plebes seem to take great measure in morality. They have an entire book of laws to live by. I have overheard some of them. They are restrictive, not to mention guilt inducing. One thing I know for certain, it was my fault she was with us in the first place. "Guilty," the words echo in my mind and I am assured that I am indeed guilty of the corruption of a servant. "I miss you Phoebe. I am sorry, so sorry." I cry out in remorse. An acute pain jabs me in my side. I am horrified. I am certain that I am missing a rib. I poke my finger into the empty space.

Before leaving I have an argument with the little humpbacked island that I can see from my perch. "Listen to me," I cry out, "before I came here I was Giulia, daughter of the great almighty Caesar Augustus, destined to rule at his right side. My father once said to me that I was his daughter with whom he was well pleased." Of course I was only ten years old and not yet corrupted. I murmur these things to myself.

The island replies that I have erroneous thinking and that promises are often made and more often not kept.

I whimper, "Is it too small a thing to ask to be pardoned and returned to my home? I have no taste for the cup that caused me to stagger, so please restore me to my garments of splendour and you will see with your own eyes my transformation."

"Your words are shallow and not authentic," the island replied.

"Never mind", I say with cruel resolve. "Are you not able to remember the passion and fire that formed you? Now you lie dormant and too complacent to rescue me." I apologize immediately, for I do not mean to be so harsh or cruel, plus I do not wish to be rebuked. "I shall go mad if we continue this conversation." I tell the island. "I am leaving."

Exile does devious things to one's mind, and with each passing thought I am convinced of a plan likely inspired by Livia out of exasperation with our failed marriage. Our union was meant to enforce our family's destiny to rule Rome. It simply was not working according to Livia's plan. Her quest for power was conspired in the first place to bring Tiberius into an exulted position as Augustus' second in command. I doubt this will come to fruition since my father has aspirations for my sons Gaius and Lucius. I need not worry about Tiberius because he is incompetent and will prove this on his own volition. Furthermore, he has no desire for the position. As for myself, I needed to be removed before I scandalize the imperial household. Plotting, scheming, and intrigue around every corner is a way of life that I was entertained by, but one that I had no intentions of being the recipient of. I definitely made some serious errors in judgment, and then I ask myself who might possibly care now if I am remorseful or not. I end my reverie of impractical solutions and suspicious plots with firm resolve that I do not like people in general, nor do I trust them, although I admit that I do miss them.

Feeling guilty about disliking humanity, on the way back to the villa I make a mental list of the people that I actually do like. I resolve that I shall strive to be more like Damaris, even if she is just a servant. You will never catch her brooding, although I have witnessed her pondering at times. There is a difference, I think to myself. In the future I shall learn to ponder these things in my heart. My poor thoughts are causing vexations of the spirit.

"Emulate the wise man: even if you cannot acquire 'his' skills, at least you can acquire some of 'his' habits", Tiberius voice echoes in my head. I defiantly change it to "Emulate the wise person: even if you cannot acquire 'her' skills, at least you can acquire some of Damaris' habits." Perhaps, I shall acquire some of Mishma's elusiveness while I am at it. Conversations with my own self have become a way of life. Too bad I am so argumentative; furthermore, I am uncertain if only one person can have a conversation.

I miss Ovid. I admired him and his bizarre creative thoughts on life. That fateful night he was at his best. Wisely, as is his habit, he left the party early. I have to save this for another day, for I have tired myself out and need a rest, just like the earth needs to rest, so Dilf tells me.

There are no intellectual challenges here on this island. I do miss them. Long ago, when I was no longer allowed to join in the young men's philosophical discussions, Tiberius informed me in his arrogant manner that it was because I was just a girl and had to learn to do the things that would make me a good wife. I recall how incensed I was, how I stuttered and stammered out my indignation and how this in turn pleased him, immensely, since he had found a weak point in my countenance. Thereafter, he used the phrase frequently, just to pluck my tail feathers. Now, I chastise myself for thinking of Damaris as just a servant. She is more than that. She is becoming a friend. This will take time. We have wounds to mend. She mothers Dilf. I change my previous thinking to embrace Damaris as a treasured servant with more authenticity in her soul than any of the aristocracy.

There is no one here to correct me, like Livia or Scribonia, who were always quick with their criticism. Who would ever have guessed that I would miss that? I did not take well to criticism, bristling literally with hair raising response, but remembering and learning, unfortunately only taking what suited me and discarding the rest with reckless abandon.

Spent now, I collapse on the stone bench. "My place knows me no more", I am muttering and blubbering. My weakness sickens me. I feel pathetically small. The hand of the oppressor delivers a crushing pain to my chest, leaving me immobile. Maybe I am dreaming, I just do not know. Fortunately, Mishma has come along, for my legs will not carry me back to the villa. I cannot move and know not why. Mishma wraps me in a dark grey woolen shawl. Supporting me, he guides me gently back to the garden in the centre of the villa. Soon enough I will be clothed in darkness and grateful for the long shadow which heralds the day's end.

* * * * * * * * *

"Help me!" The Epicurean poet, Lucretius embraces me, soothing my agony. He fingers the tear in the curtain, and then rents it in two, exposing the gap between birth and death. The sun caresses my face and warms my body. The poet needs a new sole for his sandals. Mishma provides one. Moonbeam smiles. The dog is a sailor: wind and freedom are his companions.

Morning light pokes through a small tear in the curtain.

"I am dying." I cry out. "Send a letter to Rome. Request my return, so I might die peacefully in the comfort of my own bed".

I have difficulty swallowing. My air passage constricts causing a rattle called "Death". Damaris holds my head up and provides me with sips of water while Dilf places cold cloths on my forehead. They tell me I have slept for days. It is obvious they are confused, for it was only yesterday that Mishma carried me back to the garden. They look haggard, like they could use a good night's sleep.

"Death comes as fast as burnt offerings," I tell them earnestly. "Death tastes of bitter herbs; it has the rhythm of a poem of lament, and the incessant sound of the ocean. Its touch is crushing. Look, you can see its vapour lurking behind the tear in the curtain."

Damaris and Dilf look at me, condescendingly, as if I do not know what I am talking about. I ask Dilf if she might listen for my heartbeat. She puts her ear to my chest and listens intently. Dilf confirms that I remain in the between time.

I close my eyes trying my best to conjure up death's colour. It is as nondescript as light on a shadow.

VII

Damaris, called to be a servant of the Roman Empire,

To Livia

We, your servants, thank you for the privilege of serving Rome.

In regards to Giulia, she seems to be in shock. I say this on behalf of the three of us, as we have noticed that she is not responding to her exile with tears, anger or other emotions. There is just a silence that gives us cause for concern.

Daily she walks to the steps leading down to the cistern and sits there for hours. Dilf or Mishma fetch her, for we fear she will not return on her own and become ill with the chills or succumb to the darkness of the shades.

Giulia eats meagrely and has to be coaxed. Her hair is brittle, her skin is pallid, and her eyes are dim.

We do our best to keep her engaged in conversation, but mostly she is unresponsive.

Our hearts go out to her. If you have any suggestions, your guidance would be appreciated.

I submit this letter at the end of our first month in exile.

Peace and grace be unto you.

VIII

Livia, wife of Caesar Augustus, called to be a councillor of Rome,

To: Damaris and Company

As you well know, it is a privilege we have bestowed on you to serve Rome.

We trust Giulia into your care and expect you to do the best you can in the circumstances given.

Regards from the palace of Caesar Augustus

IX

Black flies buzz around my head. I try to swat them away, but there are too many. Tiberius appears on the steps leading up to the tribunal. He pushes me. I stumble and push him back. He falls down the stairs. A giant hand casts a shadow over my being, and then people begin to throw stones at me. As I fall to the ground, I duck, cringe, and curl into a fetal position while protecting my head with my hands. A large boulder is about to strike.

I awaken with a jolt, as if struck by the boulder. The dream triggers unwanted memories. Again and again, I relive past hurts and embarrassing times. Memory takes me back to yet another morning with its aftereffects from over indulgence. I digress to the afternoon of yet another medal ceremony where Tiberius and others would be bestowed with honours for their victorious battles and for their contribution towards the betterment of Roman society. Tiberius had been awarded a badge of honour and crowned with a victory wreath for his legion's victory at Illyricum. I recall how smart he looked in his bordered tunic, but the laurel wreath sitting on his head was slightly askew. I remember that when I instinctively reached over to straighten the wreath he batted my hand away like it was a pesky fly.

Later that day, as the honoured were paraded through the streets, Berenice had told me that Tiberius saw his former wife Vipsania and broke into tears and wept openly, for all to see. I tried to convey a look of nonchalance. Deep inside, my guts were writhing in anguish.

The next evening there was to be a banquet. During the day, I had gone through the motions of preparing for the banquet. Diana, a woman known for her adeptness, created my notorious hair dressing, one that was too complex to become the fashion of the day, but one that was talked about for days. She had asked what I had in mind, and I had replied that she might do as she wished. "See if you can raise my spirits", I had replied, without really meaning it, for I was feeling insignificant. Diana had responded with enthusiasm. Many hours later, I had a hairstyle that brought a genuine smile to my face. So totally absurd was her creation, it will be difficult to describe such splendour. But I will try, knowing I will not be able to do it justice.

I smile as I look into the mirror, barely recognizing the image starting back at me as my own. First of all, framing my face and the nape of my neck were tiny curls, the curls on the right all facing towards the centre of the forehead and the ones on the left facing towards the centre. On the crown just behind the row of curls she set a curved shield about 8 inches high. It feels heavy. My neck muscles are put to good use. Slightly larger perfectly formed curls, from my own hair and from extensions, covered the shield. A form in the shape of a cone was added just behind the shield extending back and outwards about twelve inches. A series of braids resembling fishtails covered the cone. The coiffure was finished off with three rows of tiny braids coiled in a spiral around the base of the cone. All these elaborate plaits and curls were secured with beads and a foul smelling lacquer. I smell like a dead chicken. It was painful sitting for so long, but I then endured yet one more hour having my face chalked by the cosmetician who accentuated my eyes with ash and defined my lips with red stain from berries. The overall effect is stunning.

With spirits uplifted, I recall choosing a simple white shift with a diaphanous silk cloak from India. The silk would flow like Ovid's words. I chose my jewelry with great care: first of all the dolphin earrings gifted to me by my friend Berenice to symbolize our friendship; next, clear glass beads in an ornate silver setting for my necklace; and then lastly, a clasp made of elegant pearls and glass beads to fasten the cloak at my shoulder. Intuitively, I had known that the dress should not detract from the hairdo.

Making my entrance into the dining hall with all the regal posture I could muster, I could not help but notice the pleasurable reaction. Livia and Augustus gave nods of parental approval. I was well pleased with Augustus' attentive gaze. He looked proud, as did my two sons Gaius and Lucius sitting by his side. Berenice looked in my direction arching her one eyebrow, as was her fashion. It seemed that all heads were turned towards me, giving me the attention I was so desperately needing; that is, all but one. I remember clearly that Tiberius stayed focused on his conversation with his guests. When he finally looked my way, he looked up at my dressed hair, lowered his head while peering at me from the top of his eyes. He did not move one muscle on his face, not in delight or in disgust. Indifference is what his expression registered. All too quickly, he returned to his conversation, never glancing my way again. There were times, I must confess, when I had un-wifely thoughts. Shoving him down the stairs would bring great satisfaction. But, unfortunately, lately my reaction had been to become overwhelmingly fatigued. I would be filled with apathy for days after, not to mention a headache which I am not certain was caused entirely from tension.

I had managed to stay at the banquet an appropriate length of time, taking a little solace in a cup or two of wine.

The next day, after the banquet, I made my way to the sacred grove, a place where no one would find me and where I might feel protected by the spirit of the place. Ironically, it was our hiding place, the one Tiberius and I fancied we had discovered as children, a place where we could go when great secrecy was required. Behind the curved wall of the theatre's stage, there is still a path, that we as children had imagined was forged by us. I dimly recall a time when the land was once a grove of olive trees, cleared for the building of the theatre and the paths and roads that now lead to it. Several rows of olive trees remain behind the path providing privacy. Tiberius and I had tried with all our childhood might to move a garden bench there, but we were unsuccessful. With great cunning and secrecy, we confiscated two chairs from the senate chamber and carried them to our new found hiding place. In retrospect, I suppose we were not so cunning after all and were quite likely a source of entertainment, perhaps as engaging as the great performances enacted on stage.

It was there that I sat, on a weathered chair, nursing my wounded spirit, weeping for the humiliation felt deep within. I wept for my childish need for approval, I wept for unwanted feelings of deep hatred and bitterness, and last but not least of all, I wept for our ugly relationship.

Much later, with tears well spent and some semblance of normalcy restored, to my surprise Tiberius found me and sat down beside me. Neither one of us spoke. This was as close as we ever came to being a couple.

We both tried to make our relationship a little better after that. I became pregnant, but the child was stillborn. We were going to name him Aquila. Shortly after, Tiberius departed for the island of Rhodes and his self-imposed exile.

From this day on I was no longer a semblance of what I once was, no longer able to even recognize myself or accept the things I had done, the harm I had caused or the frivolous life I had led. I used to think of this as the worst time of my life, filled with such unhappiness and such a sense of unworthiness. I had no desire for the things that used to give me pleasure. If I had succumbed to this state of morbidity, I likely would have been better off.

The styled hair that had given me a renewed sense of wellbeing was short-lived. My weakness of character and dependence on approval shames me now, but that is the way it was.

"It is what it is." I found myself reciting one of my mother's pithy quotes. I proceeded to take solace in wine and lovers, finding the wine was often more seductive and attentive than the lovers. Soon enough, the elixir not only soothed my anxieties but it loosened my inhibitions. The rest would soon be history. I suppose I was fortunate that my punishment was exile and not stoning.

With a swish of my hand, I bat away a pesky black fly.

Damaris — whose name means heifer

X

Damaris, a servant of the Roman Empire

To Livia,

Giulia is faring better than she was the first months of exile. This is reflected in her uncharacteristic brooding nature. It is at least a response.

Her hair remains dull and brittle, which is an indication of poor health. Dilf treats her hair with olive oil followed with a chamomile tea rinse. It will take many treatments and better nourishment to restore it to its original lustre.

As for nourishment, she eats like a bird, pecking away while discarding the crusts from the bread. She has a taste for olives, which gives us hope that her appetite is returning.

We still have concerns for her well-being and believe there is a possibility that she will go mad if we do not do something to relieve her loneliness. Would it be possible for Giulia to accompany us to market?

Her behaviour given the circumstances is commendable.

Peace and grace to you.

It takes a very long time to compose these letters to Livia, and time is something that we servants do not have an abundance of. Being encouraged to model Livia's script adds to the slowness. What does she think this is? A scriptorium! There is much work to be done in a day and only the three of us to do it. It is not just that I am slow of hand with the script, but prudence requires that we do not write the things that we really would like to say.

First of all, it would be a relief to tell Livia that this punishment is cruel and unreasonable. A world without a supportive community is even difficult for us servants, and we have a lot to do to occupy our minds and hands in a day.

Giulia, before the exile, was such a vibrant person. Even though we do not understand the Roman way of living, it was plain to see that she was energized by people. Giulia loved the plays, the gambling and the musical performances. Entertainment was always available. The Roman elite were generally a captive audience, laughing or crying in the appropriate places, and all the while sitting like lazy cats perched on a ledge, soaking it all in. This is unfair, and I know it, but the letters put me in a foul mood. As for the three of us servants, solitude suits us to a degree, but, admittedly, we do look forward with great anticipation to market day. We hope Livia grants us permission to take Giulia with us to the town square. There really would not be any risk in this, especially if there are no ships in harbour.

One thing that is bothersome (well, actually there are many grievances) is that Giulia does not eat her crusts, furthermore she leave a mess on her plate. When I stated in the letter to Livia that she ate like a bird, it was more in keeping with the messiness of the scattered bits and pieces of the food left to waste.

These are just a few of the things that are pondered in my heart and were not included in the letter. Well, enough of that. Anyway, no one is listening. Thank goodness! The bread has risen and needs tending to.

Dilf – whose name means buttercup

XI

The chameleon has the power to change its own colour in order to blend into its surroundings. It has the ability to pick up vibrations with its tongue. It can regenerate extremities that are lost in battle, and yet through all this it appears wizened and quite handsome in an intriguing kind of way.

If there were a creature that I should like to emulate, it would be the chameleon. Its flitting acerbic tongue spits out venom to those who vex its spirit. This is something I secretly wish for, but the truth is I am quite meek, complacent and slow to anger. Both the lizard and I amble through life, which suits me fine, but I acknowledge that it irritates others.

My name means Buttercup. This was my father's pet name for me. Others call me Dilf, short for Delphinium. The censor could not spell correctly, hence, my official name is Dilf. It suits me fine. I like Buttercup, also.

Not far from Rome lies the coastal town of Ostia, where my family hails from. Ostia's main source of income is the mining of salt. The flat coastal area has a gentle terrain that slopes towards the sea, making it ideal for the salt mining industry. The mines only operate in the hot months from May to October. My father and brothers work in the salt mines. The rest of the year, my father makes rope, and because he is so industrious, he also makes belts from the leftover hemp. My mother and I dye the belts and make soap. Still with all our hard work, we have a difficult time living within our means.

I have six brothers and sisters, four older and two younger, and parents who disagree over anything and everything. Both my parents have peculiar ways; my mother clicks her teeth and scrunches up her nose as if to indicate that she has been insulted when she is irritated and responds with a verbal "woof". Unbeknownst to her, she has a habit of mimicking others' gestures and facial expressions, which entertains us, and I am afraid to say, we mock this habit when not in her presence. Our father rules with an iron hand. We have so many rules it causes your head to spin in circles like the top he carved for us children. If a door is left open and he thinks it ought to be closed he is barely able to function until that door comes to a close. If we are to go anywhere, we must be ready and waiting or we will be left behind. One barely has time to respond to his demands or to think through an answer before he is demanding to be answered or barking orders. Small things irritate him. He can be most unreasonable, especially with us children who often cannot keep up with the demands and also, with our mother who does not concern herself with the small details as he would like her to do. In fairness to her she has too many chores to spend time on the small matters. On the other hand, our father can be quite entertaining with stories from his childhood and generous when he has the means and is not over extended.

My brothers and sisters are all so different from one another it is difficult to imagine that we were all brought up in the same household. My oldest brother is most like our father and is easily vexed, perhaps because he is the oldest and feels entitled to control the rest of us. Yet another brother is quite the opposite, being most cheerful and good natured. Two of the others are lazy and seem like they never have enough sleep. This is a possibility, since we all share two sleeping mats that are not quite large enough to accommodate us all. The two youngest, who are girls, bring us all together with their needs. The youngest girl is intelligent beyond her years, always asking questions, and is the only one who gets on well with our father, mostly because he believes she gets her cleverness from him. Mother says that it is too bad she was not a boy as her intelligence could then be put to good use. Even though she is much younger than me, she is my teacher. I learn a great deal from her, especially her love of imitating grownups words. I do admit that most often, I cannot grasp the meaning, but certainly, would never admit to my ignorance. Still I make it a practice to search for the context which is not an easy thing to do when your time is taken up with constant chores. I do not seem to draw the same kind of delight and appreciation as she does when I mimic her words.

As for myself, I am always ready to lend a helping hand, especially if given an outdoor chore. It is good to get away from the persistent whining, snivelling, gossiping, and tedious household chores. I have a better attitude towards life if given a dose of fresh air.

It has been said that all roads lead to Rome, and this is how I ended up on that road. My story is short and not coated with honey. Our taxes were overdue on my father's business. Making rope for the fishermen was seasonal. As I said before, he was industrious and used the left over twine to make belts to sell at the market when the fishermen were not able to cast their nets. Nothing was put to waste. We had no means to raise the funds that were overdue, along with the new levy. Even the best business person would find this a challenge. My father says that it costs money to build all those roads, and it has to come from someone. As my father looked at all his children one by one it seems that I was the most expendable. There was a look of relief from my siblings followed by an embarrassing shuffling of feet and downcast eyes. I am pleased to be of service to my family, but the truth is my heart was horribly bruised, and my gut was in a knot twisted as securely as a heraldic knot. Its tightening grip extends all the way to my back. Even today, if I think back on this time that knot returns, like it never left, just waiting for a memory to trigger its return. My father used this type of knot to fasten the belts that he made. Three years servitude in exchange for taxes paid in full: that is my worth.

    I was placed as a servant in the Imperial household, which made my parents feel better about their decision. At first I was given menial tasks in the kitchen, but unfortunately I was exasperatingly slow. I was then sent to fetch milk and churn butter. I was quite adept at this. It was indeed my good fortune that the lazy boy employed before me, who kept the barn, was sent out to the fields to shepherd the sheep. I now had the added task of milking the cows. Before they could replace the boy I took it upon myself to clean the barn, brush the cows and shovel the dung. There is nothing sweeter than the smell of a clean barn and nothing sweeter than the taste of milk freshly squeezed from the udder. Generally, this is not a girl's job, but it seemed to go unnoticed. I certainly did not make a show of cleaning the barn. I suppose it might be possible that this was not a task that might appeal to everyone. I constantly had to remind myself to churn the butter, so taken up was I with the cows and the barn. I did not want to jeopardize my position, which I value highly. My job is quite satisfying, and I am proud of the work I do.

    Abigail, named after my clever little sister, was my favourite cow. I was able to see her grow from a playful, adorable calf to a good natured gentle cow. I remember her as a young calf scrunched on her forelegs preparing to bunt me. After she was born she was quick to get on her feet and quick to suck. She had good hooves with no cracking. She waited patiently while I milked the five others. Pustola, the other calf born of another cow, was slow to get on her feet and needed coaxing to suck. A slight limp, likely caused by split hooves, made her surly in nature. She was irritating, like a pimple, reminding me of my older brother. I tried to be compassionate with her, but she was arrogant and pushy, demanding to be milked first. She seemed to resent my presence even though I was the one to ease her discomfort and provide her with a clean environment, fresh food and plenty of water. We argued a lot.

The other four cows were already here, so I addressed them as "Girl". I would not want to confuse them, just in case that boy gave them a name, which is doubtful. He did leave me with a gift and that was a bad case of fleas. My hair was cropped off very short. I cursed the lye soap that burns the skin, but kills the fleas. There is a possibility that it is forgotten that I am a girl. I hope that this is not so. I stick out my tiny breasts to reassure myself. Brown and cream are the colours of my tunic and cloak. They are tied with a yellow rope sash which my father braided for me. I blend in splendidly with my working environment.

As for my looks, aside from short cropped hair, I have tan freckled skin. I am not very large. Well, okay, I am small, but I am strong.

One day after delivering the milk to the kitchen, I lingered just a minute too long. I was ordered to spend some time with Giulia the Younger who was always in need of supervision. Although she is close to seventeen years, she is very childlike, prone to temper tantrums, or crying at the least provocation. You could just manage to get her on an even keel when something else would set her off. You have never witnessed such a one as that. I think there must be something wrong with her, so agitated in spirit does she become. We played games and I let her win at dice to put her in a better mood. I combed her hair and plaited it, tying it with coloured ribbons which helped to placate her. Perhaps, you might think me hard hearted, but I seldom cry myself and am more intrigued by Giulia the Younger's dramatic performance of wailing and sulking than I am sympathetic. I might cry if a tree were cut down or if one of my cows were suffering, but I seldom weep over the human condition.

Damaris, Livia's house maid, came to my rescue in the afternoon. Damaris has a limp that causes her to be slow in pace, but it does not affect her demeanor like that arrogant old cow, Pustola. Damaris' working pace is steady and efficient, not hurried, but she gets as much done, if not more, with this steady measured pace. She is a quiet woman and so am I. I suppose this is why we are comfortable with one another. We both seem to know that you can make a connection without constant chatter. Even though I do not care to work at indoor chores, I try and do my best for Damaris, for she is someone I desire to please.

Now for reasons unbeknownst to me, but for which I am grateful, Damaris has recommended that I accompany her into exile. As my father signed a contract for three years of servitude, and I have completed two years of this obligation, the choice has been left up to me to decide whether to work out the other year here or go to Pandateria for five years. I have chosen to accept, as truthfully, I am wont to admit, I dread returning to my family because I am so ashamed for being so expendable. The fact that Damaris chose me is sufficient reason for me to accept her offer.

So here I am exiled on the island of Pandateria. I really like it here, as there are not so many people. City life is not for me. I actually have more freedom than even Giulia who is confined to the villa and its grounds. When Giulia is not sleeping she cries a lot. Even when she is sleeping you can hear her moans and lamentations. I know I should be more sympathetic to her plight but her constant wailing and gnashing of teeth is tedious. I truly was relieved that she was not stoned to death. Some folks thought this an appropriate punishment. That would be horrid. I cringe at the thought of it and duck as the imaginary stones strike my body. Like my mother, I mimic Giulia's sad expressions so she might think I am sympathetic to her condition. Sometimes, to help Damaris out, I comb and plait Giulia's hair. It worked for her daughter, so I hope it might help her also, but mostly I do it to ease Damaris' workload.

I spend a good part of my day foraging to supplement our simple diet. Sometimes, Tiberius does not send Giulia's allowance, and it is then my skills come in handy. I take pleasure from the feeling of greediness that overwhelms me when there is an abundance of berries, ripe on the vine, ready for plucking. It causes me to salivate in anticipation of the treat Damaris will concoct from my contribution. Bacchus would be overjoyed by my lack of control. I know I am.

We have a goat here on the island, as opposed to a cow. I need to work on this relationship; so far we are at odds. All and all, I am well pleased with my lot in life. At this time and place, my needs are met.

XII

Livia, wife of Caesar Augustus, called to be a councillor of Rome

To: Damaris and company

Permission is not granted. Let me remind you that we trust Giulia into your care and expect you to do the best you can in the circumstances given.

I have important matters to tend to and have no time for responding to requests that ought not to be placed on my shoulders.

Regards from the palace of Caesar

"I also have important matters to tend to." I respond to Livia's letter by stretching my neck, turning up my nose and arrogantly nodding my head from side to side as if I were the Queen of Sheba herself.

Damaris - whose name means heifer

XIII

Most people fear exile, some even go insane and the odd one like Tiberius welcomes it, as I also do. It will not be a hardship for me to leave the Imperial household and the bustling city of Rome, the people and all that goes with their lifestyle. Everyone seems to be in a hurry, constantly demanding attention. The lust for blood-filled entertainment is discouraging, to say the least. I vomit if I think about their pathetic idea of sport. Betrayal even amongst family members is perplexing, for I consider home to be a place of refuge. Most disconcerting is the constant noise. Neither will I miss Livia, since she was a demanding taskmaster: not that I minded for the days pass more quickly when one is occupied. Busyness leaves little time for fear or sorrow or dwelling on one's misfortunes. Livia was also impatient with my clumsy foot, which slowed me down. I tried in vain to muffle the dragging sound of my noncompliant foot but the more I tried the slower I moved, so I had to choose efficiency over insulting her sensibilities. Her constant eye-rolling, pursing of lips, shaking of her head, and also her constant criticism which she tried to disguise as kindly advice, was a source of irritation for me. I was not in the position to voice my concerns. I knew her gestures to be contemptuous in nature. I was not the only recipient. Livia often lamented that she should have brought me a pair of stealth booties from some far away land called the Orient. All too often, I was reminded that my affliction could be construed as a harbinger of bad luck for the Imperial household and how fortunate I was that they kept me on. Well, it was indeed my bad luck to have my foot trampled by the Imperial horses charging into town, with no regard for others, to declare yet one more proclamation. I consider it good luck, indeed, to be leaving this all behind.

Shuffle, shuffle, stamp, is the sound of my gait. My right foot moves normally, but, try as I might, I cannot will the left one to live in compliance with the movement of the rest of my body. 'What has been done, has been done; so be it', my mother's proverb echoes from days gone by. It is fortunate that I do not have pain, well perhaps a little at the end of the day, but by then I am so tired it does not get the attention it so deserves. Really, there is so little time to ponder fortune or misfortune. I try to keep my human nature. When I do have a moment I grow rather despondent and lonely for my mother and my dear friend Phoebe. It is best if I keep myself occupied with chores.

It seems we servants are prone to bad luck. It was Phoebe's bad luck that Giulia needed her company on that fateful night. With reluctance, I will share with you that I am sometimes angry, and that anger is not only directed at Giulia but also towards my friend for taking her own life. What kind of friend am I that I should have such awful thoughts? There are endless unanswered questions, like why she did not come to me, her closest friend, and share her doubts and whatever else was troubling her so much as to take her own life? Phoebe was a gentle spirit, gullible and ever so orderly to the point where trifles had the ability to immobilize her. I could have saved her from her erroneous thinking, or at least she could have let me try. When I am not angry, I am ever so sad and miss her terribly. It is best if I just keep busy.

I pride myself on efficiency, and if you saw my matronly body you would recognize the fact that also I am a good cook. I am only eighteen years old with the body of a thirty year old. For relaxation I enjoy making rag shawls. It takes forever to complete one, since I do not have a lot of spare time.

I come from Krenidi, a small village on the Peloponnese. Our family lived in a small stone house, nice and cool in the summer and warm in the winter. The most interesting part of the home for us children was the cellar. Behind the storage area, there was a crystal cave which we were to stay away from. It was not navigable and was dark as Hades. As children we loved to hear the echo of our voices, but we kept our distance, fearing the dark pit of the abyss. I carry with me a crystal from that cave; otherwise I might cease to believe that it ever existed. There were only four of us in the family: my brother Elias, my mother and father, as well as myself. I remember the lemon tree in the courtyard, with its delicious tangy fruit in such abundance that it was not uncommon to squeeze ten or even twenty onto the roasting lamb, which was sprinkled with a generous amount of course salt. Of course, this was only a once or twice per year occasion, but one that I shall never forget, with each of us taking our turns at the spit. Quite often the roasting would happen on May Day, which was also the day we celebrated the May birthdays, mine being one of them.

This is a memory that warms my heart. I can still taste those pungent lemons as acrid as Livia's criticism. Even though Rome is not that far away, there are no lemons here that compare in flavour. I smile as I recall the look on Elias' face as he sucked on the fruit, making his ridiculously funny, fish face. Lemons, crystals and motherly love; that is all I can recall, but sometimes, it grieves me to say that sometimes I forget what my family looked like. It is then that I feel sorry for my misfortune. This happened one day after picking a basket of those very lemons to take to the Wednesday market in Ermione, a small sea port on the southern part of the isle. My life as I knew it was over in the flash of an instant. I often ask myself why Roman soldiers would even bother with such a small town. I am still perplexed, not to mention traumatized. My father went to market with me to purchase an item, that which I have forgotten. Every once in a while, I dwell on this like it is the most important memory ever, but I am unable to come up with the answer. Even so, I search and I search, but the answer remains elusive. At the marketplace, my father and I went our separate ways. I do not know what became of him, but I pray constantly that he was able to return to my mother and at least tell her of my abduction. I was twelve years old at the time and getting uncomfortably close to betrothal. If I had known what I know now, I would have welcomed it, but the truth is I lived in dread of having to leave my family, even if I remained in the same village. Worse yet, I worried that I might have to move away. Then I would concern myself with whom I might marry, and if he would be kindly or brutish, but mostly I worried that he might not be clean and that he might smell like horse manure.

Instead, I now have new unimagined worries. It is a goal for Caesar Augustus that all roads will lead to Rome, and this is how I arrived here. I have spent the past six years in the Imperial household. Some say this is an honoured position. I suppose it could have been worse, but I rather doubt it.

Daily, I thanked God for my friend Phoebe. She was a spark of light in an otherwise intolerable situation. We helped each other survive the demands of our betters often with humour and wicked mimicry, which only reminds me that I cannot recall the last time that I laughed or had some semblance of happiness. Phoebe taught me to plait hair, since this was now the current fashion, and my position of serving Livia required me to be adept at all these things. Livia's demands kept me on my toes, five of them anyway. I lacked many of the skills required, such as hairdressing, applying women's colours and coordinating outfits. Phoebe was adept and shared her expertise, which really was mostly practicing being patient with those who were impatient. Back home we had two colours that I can recall: tea coloured linen and grey wool. Here there is such an array of fabric and coloured sashes, it would make your head spin. The choices confound me. In the end, it really does not matter, since Livia will choose something other than what I have suggested. Augustus dresses simply and without flare, but he likes his women to make up for his simplicity of style. This seems to give him a sense of prestige. Livia's and Giulia's dress, elaborate hair styles and exotic jewelry become reflections of his refined taste.

I must say that Livia has a style of her own. On the other hand, Giulia often got caught up with the latest trends, succumbing to the enticement of imported silks and dyes, and changing her style like a chameleon changes its colours. Livia keeps her dress refined and classical, insisting on the finest quality. She does not want for jewels, though, and she also has a taste for exotic hairstyles, preferring to set the trend rather than follow it. This is the part that is difficult for me, but with each special occasion I am improving. If I had more time, perhaps I could meet her expectations. Phoebe, as always, was my saviour, mentoring me in the latest techniques and showing me how to apply the combs and ribbons. Soon enough I was fixing combs with the best of them.

This May I shall be nineteen years old, unmarried and not likely ever to be. May Day now makes me sadder with each passing year. I realize that after five more years in exile, I will be too old to be betrothed to a younger man. Perhaps my parents, if I ever get home, will know of a widower with a family that needs nurturing. Yes, that will do nicely. Hopefully, I will not have to wed an old codger who needs care and constant attention. I pray that he might come from the same village and that he not be a drinker. After witnessing the dinner parties here, drunkenness fills me with anxiety and loathing, especially when they gorge themselves, then purge so they can eat more. It is so disgusting, you cannot begin to imagine. Besides, the smell of vomit makes me gag and the sight of it repels me to no end. I do not have the skills required to be a good nurse. I do not doubt that my mother will do what she can to keep me close to her. I pray that my father is alive. I hope Elias has a wife and two or more fat babies. I doubt that I shall ever return. I cannot see how this could possibly happen. Even as a Libertine, I would not have the means to get home. It is best not to think about such things as the future.

But May Day will not oblige and leave my thoughts. Memory takes me to the countryside only a short distance from our village. We walk along the stream as we watch and listen to water rippling over stones. We help the elders cross the brook as we wend our way back to the picnic site where we listen to the musicians, dance and tell stories. An elder chants the evening prayers to mark the end of day. I remember that those prayers seemed way more meaningful when mingling with fresh air and the quiet murmurings of contented folks.

I would like to have shared these May Day memories with Phoebe. Even though she has heard me reminiscing before, she always listened attentively. It is rare to find a person who actually listens. At the feasts in this household, everyone talks and no one listens, unless of course Augustus is speaking, but even then I am not so sure they are really attentive or just patiently waiting to get back to their own chatter and zest-filled indulgences. I am not even certain that they taste what they are eating. They could learn a lesson or two from Dilf's cows. It appears that the guests do not know the meaning of savour. I suppose it is because they have too many choices and are impatient to experience them all at once. I suppose that I should not be so harsh in my criticism. Perhaps, if I were reared in this custom, I might be no better. I must try to be more compassionate and mend my way of thinking. I am aware that I can be judgmental.

And now my life turns to exile on the island of Pandateria. I welcome leaving the bustle of Roman life, which I found disagreeable. The constant noise made it difficult to think about the tasks at hand. The excessive desire for frivolous adventure like shopping and gambling showed a flagrant disregard for those who work long hours for their wages. Worst of all, the lust for blood at the arena truly vexes my spirit. The spikes on the chariot wheels are sharpened knives which injure the animals and lop off the limbs of humans as quickly as flailing grain. I fail to comprehend how this might excite someone. I am grateful that I cannot understand this act of cruelty that is so indifferent to suffering. I had to plead with Livia to be exempted from accompanying her to these bloody events. Fortunately for me, she understood my plight and was uncharacteristically sympathetic, allowing me to remain behind with promises of putting my time to good use.

The quietude of an island is something I look forward to. Mishma seems adept. I think he will be an asset to the household, although I am ashamed to say that the odour that comes from him is truly offensive. I shall pray that my facial expressions never give me away and that I shall not gag as I am prone to do. Dilf is not very competent regarding indoor chores but more than makes up for it if she is given anything to do outdoors. She has healing skills that will likely come in handy. She is a homely child, which only increases my fondness for her.

Of course there will be Giulia to care for. She is considered to be a beautiful woman with a voluptuous full body, big sensual pouty lips, and a flamboyant and flirtatious personality. None of her outward features appeals to me, but I feel kindly towards her generous and benevolent character. I feel sorry for her privileged life, which has not allowed her character to deepen. And now this harsh punishment might be too much for such an advantaged person to bear. I shall try very hard not to despise her for the part she played in Phoebe's death. In my mind I know that she is a product of her environment, but in my heart I sometimes have troubling feelings.

Dilf – whose name means buttercup

XIV

Mishma's name means "One Who Hears". There never was a person more aptly named. Mishma is not one for conversation. I have heard him babbling away to the birds and mimicking their calls. Otherwise he does not have much to say.

Bit by bit, Mishma has told me his story as I nursed his wound, which was not any easy task with the stench from the botched operation being of the foulest nature and the putrid pus oozing out his anger with unabashed hatred. I would make the poultice, and Mishma would apply it, for he is a modest man. I would dispose of the viscid soaked old poultice, but not before I had a good look at it, since I needed to see if there was improvement. I tried in vain not to be disdainful, but that was difficult. People keep their distance from Mishma, and for good reason, because his odour is as putrid as his sore. This was quite likely the reason he was sent here. We exiles all had a good reason for our banishment. I am a dolt, so they say. I have been told this many times, so I know why I am here. It is obvious why Mishma is here, and we all know why Giulia is here. The reason for Damaris' presence is a conundrum, for she is the most efficient person and the most benevolent soul I have ever met. I suppose it is because of her supposedly ill-omened lame foot, but I can honestly say there is nothing ill-omened about Damaris in any way. She is angelic in my eyes, and I am a good judge of character. More so, I am a better judge of cows rather than humans, but nevertheless I think she is a good person.

Today the pus is thick and greenish yellow, but not as dark and sticky as it started out. There is a slight improvement, but not in the smell.

Mishma tells me he is from Nubia in the upper Nile Region. Mishma has black curly hair, cut very short with a receding hair line. He has eyes that seem to focus inward rather than on the outward things of this world. This is difficult to explain, but he seldom gives direct eye contact, and yet he sees all. His other senses must be very acute, since his skills at servitude are exceptional. Mishma has fine high cheekbones, full lips and a protruding chin. His neck is long, and he has a disciplined posture that imputes a sense of dignity. Mishma dresses in a homespun tunic, worn thin from washing. When it is cool, he wears a light cloak tied with an aubergine knot with dangling threads. I mean to ask him about this. I suspect it has to do with a memory from home. I suppose it is best that I do not ask, as Mishma is a private man. He will tell me if it needs telling.

This much I know. His mother's name is Maryan, and his father's name is Mesfin. I think of them as harmonious, I guess because their names sound good together. Maryan and Mesfin, I repeat the names to myself. Mishma remembers his father as always being impeccably groomed. Mesfin would go to the town square daily to deal with the problems of the people, which were always many. He was treasurer, tax collector, administrator and scribe. These were but a few of his duties. Mishma learned these worldly skills from his father, who was a tradesman proficient in reading and accounting. His younger brother Nigel was most often attached to Mishma's left side, or so it seemed.

Then there was Ainy.

Mishma pleaded, "Dilf, please do not ask me about her ever again. I will tell you this once and only once."

According to Mishma, Ainy was the most beautiful girl ever, with the most beautiful smile ever. Her positive outlook on life was as infectious as her smile. Her eyes, he continued, danced like sunlight on water. Children were drawn to her, often walking out of their way just to be by her side. We dreamed of being surrounded with the joy and pleasure of many little ones.

Silence ensued.

Mishma continued and spoke of the night of their betrothal, when Ainy wore a purple dress with an embroidered hem of red, orange and blue flowers. Under the base of the neckline were three round medallions of red, blue and white in a 'V' formation. The diaphanous burgundy shawl draped over her head, seemed to embrace her. Mishma told me that every time he poured wine for the Romans he would think of that shawl, for it was the same deep colour. He carried on with his vivid description remembering all the minute details down to an adornment of shiny leaves with a shimmering border. Draped around her beautiful black hair was a shiny silvery-white hair band with its points facing downward resting gently on her beautiful forehead. Mishma placed the mark of a 'V' on his forehead. He told me Ainy was not very tall. I reflected that neither is Mishma, even though he has the appearance of a tall person because of his erect posture. He began to describe the sandals worn on his beloved's feet, but his emotions got the best of him. He whispered to me that she was so beautiful.

"So very beautiful", I added.

I left Mishma with his new poultice and his own thoughts. I was amazed at his vivid description: I had never heard a man be so descriptive of a woman's dress.

Mishma – whose name means one who hears

XV

I must never speak of Ainy again. Not to humans, anyway. The birds keep it to themselves. I know Dilf will share what I have told her with Damaris. I am grateful for this, since I will not have to relive this painful memory.

My thoughts turn to the afternoon the Roman soldiers came. I had gone with my father to the town square. Father sent me to the baker's stall for our free allotment of bread. I recall salivating over the smell of the freshly baked bread just out of the wood burning oven. I breathed deeply of the yeasty smell. The baker dusted the top with a little extra corn meal, making me feel special. Only too late, I realized I was doomed. Like a lamb being led to slaughter, my life as I knew it was over, fast as the slashing of the butcher's knife. The Roman soldiers charged through the market whisking me into unknown territory.

I became a slave in the household of Octavian, the Roman emperor.

Then unspeakable horror followed and now I can only say that I am a remnant of what I once was. I became but a dry tree, and worst of all I stunk. No perfume could camouflage the putrid smell coming from what were once my vital parts. I, Mishma, am now a eunuch. Even if I ever escaped or were set free, my life with my beautiful Ainy will never be. I will never be able to speak of my descendants. As the lamb before the shearer is silent, I rage; but words do not come from my mouth. I weep tears that never flow.

As a result of these hideous inflictions, for some unknown reason every sense in my body has awakened. It has been a trial to overcome this, but I work at not letting my sense of smell overwhelm my sense of sight or my sense of touch. Most of all, my hearing has become acute. This has been on more than one occasion extremely helpful. I can hear the needs of the diners before they themselves are even aware. But what is beautiful is birdsong, which seems to me to be the only pleasure left in my life. Hearing is a safeguard for me; it gives a sense of safety and control. I need to be alert at all times so as not to be taken off guard again. Yet, even though I know it is too late and any real sense of control is futile, I still try.

The offensive smell that comes from my body invades everything. The odour from the wound gives an acrid sting to the smell of things I once was endeared to. A frequent scent that seems to attack my nostrils is the metallic smell of the forger's hammer as it strikes the anvil's block. Tea, which I have always savoured, has taken on the taste of metal. It is only the smell of bread that retains its own familiar scent. I long for this pleasure, as if it is a replacement for all that I once treasured.

My first lesson at being a slave was a harsh one. I was ordered to keep a safe distance away from the aristocracy so as not to insult their sensibilities, yet at the same time, I was to be alert to their demands and their hand signals. At the feast, some of the people were gorging themselves. In order to eat more, they would throw up in a bucket supplied by me. I was to be quick so as not to ruin other's appetites. The abundance of food was overwhelming, yet they ate like there was a scarcity. I have never seen humans eat like this. I was truly revolted. I suppose my expression gave away my feelings, for I was beaten in a demeaning manner with slaps and spat upon in front of the appreciative diners. Fortunately for me, I am now considered to be a Roman citizen. Therefore, under Roman law, I am excluded from degrading forms of punishment such as being prodded with hot rods, scourged, or punished with whips of leather with little bits of bones attached. Yes indeed, I am a fortunate man!

From that time on I would become the epitome of a dignified and efficient waiter. No gesture would escape my eye. I would be there to satisfy their whims and just as quickly retreat so as not to insult their olfactory organs.

Ironically, this foul odour emanating from my wound has brought some relief to my life. I will be exiled and allowed to serve the wayward daughter of Octavian, who incidentally, has been renamed Augustus to glorify his position as emperor. The now venerable Augustus needs to purge his household of the unwanted and the outcasts. Each one of us exiles meets this standard. After five years of serving his daughter Giulia, here on the island of Pandateria, I will become a libertine.

Now what does a freed eunuch do with a liberated life? There will be a lot of prison doors to deal with. It would take a miracle to unlock them. I simply cannot think this through. The possible solutions are as rift as the impotency of a eunuch.

To bring me solace, I finger the knotted cord from my father's cloak. When we were at the market, it had come loose. I had tucked it in my purse to give to my mother to mend when we returned home. How grateful I am for this one piece of my family. It is a cord of salvation that will help me through times of tribulation. I am a man of few possessions. This has always been so. Back home I never felt poor, for my father was rich in my eyes. I was always hungry for time with him, which was a rarity as he was needed in so many areas of community life. I was proud of his position as town clerk and the respect he received from the people of our village. He served and never complained.

It seems bakers have a way of presenting themselves to me at crucial times in my life. When I was at the market in Rome, a baker asked me to read a scroll he had in his possession. I read it slowly, as I had not read aloud in some time. He waved me off and tucked the scroll in my pocket as it apparently was of no interest to him. It is one of the few treasures I possess. The scroll speaks of a God, a single deity, not like the many gods of the Romans. This God gives messages to people like me and the prophet Isaiah. It is impossible to believe that this message was not meant specifically for me. I stand up straight and read the words aloud even though I know the words of Isaiah by heart. "Like a sheep to the slaughter and as a lamb before the shearers is silent, so he did not open his mouth. In his humiliation he was deprived of justice. Who can speak of his descendants, for his life was taken from earth."

After I speak the words, Isaiah tells me that questions hold answers just by being asked.

I ask him if he had a dream or a vision of me losing my manhood. "If you are such a holy one and such a visionary, then why did not you save me or warn me?" I continued on, "Your name means 'The Lord Saves'. Who is this Lord? How can this God deliver me from oppression? Is it not a little too late for that?"

I ask the prophet the same questions over and over. He never speaks aloud, yet he continues to discuss things with me. I know him well. It seems he knows a lot about me too. Isaiah is the only one who now speaks to me in my mother tongue. His words rest on me like the wind. He says if I keep the Sabbath he will give me an everlasting name. I refuse, because I have an honourable name. My parents gave it to me, and I am going to keep it.

Once I was a normal little boy thinking myself a man. Now I am not normal, and I know it. My most trusted companion is a dead man, as this Isaiah lived eons ago. I cling to his words. I value what little time we have together. Sometimes I doubt. Sometimes I believe. Sometimes I despair. Seldom do I hope.

Most of the time, I do not think about these things. Damaris, Dilf and I work long hours to keep the household in order. We strive for some semblance of normalcy. The winter months are difficult; I try my best to keep the fires stoked. It is not that there is more to do; it is just that when I am cold my body does not work as efficiently. There is a saying that the slave longs for the shadow. Well, that must be some privileged slave; that is all I can say. Our days last long beyond the shadow's arm. The first two years we had difficulty adjusting to the many tasks that used to be handled by more servants than just the three of us. I cannot recall anything other than labouring. I do what I can in a day.

At the end of each day, I say the prayer that my mother taught me. She was so gentle, my mother. She was also the best cook in the whole world. I was her treasured son. She told this to Nigel also. I hope he is well and still wrapped in our mother's loving arms. It pains me to say that sometimes I cannot remember her face, but I can always recall the sound of her voice uttering this prayer that I now, also, recite at the end of each day. "It has been a long day. What has been done has been done, what has not been done has not been done. Let it rest. Blessed be."

XVI

With my back pressed against the cement step, I manage to shelter myself from the wind but not from the cold, which is sending shivers up and down my spine. Moss clings to the stones of the archway as stubbornly as I cling to memories of status, the Roman community, my own bed, friends and lovers and all things lost for a cup of wine and a little romance. Wrapping my cloak a little more securely around my body, I weave a cocoon made of threads of sadness and loneliness. Today feels bleaker than other days. I fear I shall go mad.

The dark gall with its overpowering strength is pressing on my chest, making it difficult for me to breathe. This morbid state is probably a result of two recent dreams which I had hoped to dismiss. One of these could be conveniently forgotten, but two dreams with similar content need to be acknowledged, or else I shall surely drown in my own sorrow. With difficulty, I recall the dream. I am so very tired; it is a challenge to think.

> *I am handed a written proclamation of Tiberius' death. On each side of the large papyrus scroll are two life-sized prominent columns. The scroll contains a lengthy account of Tiberius' accomplishments written in blood red ink.*

This is all I can recall of the dream.

I believe after reflecting on the dream that the columns symbolize strength and support. This does not resonate with my thoughts on Tiberius' weak character. The fact that there are two columns speaks of his double-sided nature of good and evil, which for that matter all of us are made of. Therefore, one of his columns ought to have been mammoth in proportion. For some inexplicable and contradictory reason the blood red ink conjures up an image of my father's *Pax Romana*. The edict was meant to replace the bloody and triumphant might of the Roman Empire, which I suppose is now warmly ensconced in pastoral peace now that I have been removed. My thoughts turn to Tiberius, who had a lust for blood sport. I can visualize him drooling over the spilt blood of the animals and gladiators. The more they languished the more satisfied he became, hurling insults at their weakness. The blood mingles with the mud, like my thoughts and feelings, which are becoming so murky making it hard to discern the difference. I am left perplexed by too much thinking. On the one hand, there is the life force surging through the veins of the peace keepers and on the other hand there is the ebbing of life flowing out of the sacrificial victims. Perhaps I am making too much of this dream, and it is just a portent of things to come, maybe even the death of Tiberius.

The other dream seems to be connected in some confusing way.

> *Berenice appears. There is a proclamation of death. It is written on a wax tablet. The tablet lists Berenice's good deeds. She is preparing for a charitable event. I visit unannounced. She raises her one eyebrow. Berenice continues with her preparations. Berenice receives me graciously. In her own hand she etched this account onto the wax tablet. My social blunder was written for all to see.*

I flush with embarrassment as if the dream were a reality. It is evident that I visited at an inopportune time. Her raised eyebrow attests to this. This dream left me with feelings of humiliation over my boorish behaviour. All would read of my lack of social skills and once again I would be the topic of gossip.

I question the dream. "Why am I dreaming of proclamations of death?"

The augur would have suggested that I treat the dream as if it were a play, giving it a title and a plot. Now, as then, I have difficulty separating the two. Nevertheless, I try and follow his instruction from what seems like long ago.

I name the dream 'Death of a Friend'. I am feeling very sad over the implied death of my friend, so sad in fact that her death seems very real. I begin sobbing with the conviction of a professional mourner. All the traits that I have disliked in her vanish, and she becomes the epitome of all that is good in a friend. The perceived reality of her death leaves me numb with grief. I think it is a miracle that I have survived to mourn this loss. I sit for a while trying to recover from this sadness, which is very different from the loneliness I was experiencing earlier today.

I remind myself that this is only a dream and one that I did not wish to acknowledge. I try to clear my head and contemplate the purpose and message of this dream. The plot leaves me puzzled. I am not certain whether it is about Berenice's accomplishments or my humiliation. Perhaps it is about the complexity of friendship. As if they were here, I see the faces of the performers camouflaging real hurts and pain behind laughing masks. "Is that it?" I question whether our friendship was a performance and whether we were too influenced by the impact of others' expectations to get to the true meaning of friendship. I hope she is alive so we can have a second chance. Like the wax tablet in the dream, our failings could be wiped clean with a warmed stick. The scribe could re-write it until we get it right.

Over and over the same questions surface: Why have I not heard from Berenice, and why did she not say goodbye? Did our friendship not mean anything to her? Why was our friendship so complex? Why do I let Berenice and Tiberius plague my thoughts and even invade my dreams?

Even though I have come to a somewhat logical interpretation, as usual I am still feeling inadequate without the guidance of the augur. Now it is as if the augur is actually present with me, prodding and coaxing me into revelations.

The augur poses a question. "What traits did they have that you would like to emulate?" The augur does not allow me to list traits that vex me, even though I am much better at this.

I respectfully obey and tell him that Tiberius was a good orator, commanding attention from his audience not just for the content but for his infectious way of delivery. He was able to project his voice with authority, his voice rising and falling in appropriate places, with timely pauses all adding to the effectiveness of an eloquent speaker. I admire the way he entered the room, with his cloak flowing and his hurried steps. It was as if the wind were announcing his arrival. He also had a good memory for people and their deeds. I am not allowed to tell that he did not always use this information for the good of all. So, I perish the thought.

As for Berenice, she was generous and benevolent. Her dress was impeccable. Her demeanour was orderly and dignified, particularly in the company of men. She could arch one eyebrow, passing judgment more effectively than with words. As if he is present, I give the augur a sideways glance to see if it is acceptable to say 'particularly in the company of men.' He seems indifferent, so I continue. When there was just the two of us, she could be a lot of fun. We shared secrets. She was a good friend. I change that to 'she is a good friend', wanting to keep her alive.

The augur asks me what I might learn from this dream. Once again, he reminds me to think about it as if the play is over and I am now in the company of interesting people who would speculate on the underlying message of the play.

It takes a long time, but then I have lots of that.

"I think I have learned that I need to let go of my morbid attachment to these two." The augur nods in satisfaction.

I speculate on whether I have gone mad in my solitary confinement. Conversations with people from my past help pass the time, so I excuse myself. Besides, I am not certain that I give a donkey's ass. Make that an ass's ass! Livia would bristle at how uncouth I have become. So Be It!

"The moss clinging to the lifeless stone speaks more eloquently of my dream than any of my inept interpretations." The augur nods in agreement.

"Death is so lifeless," I add. "Soon enough there will just be me and the sea and a vast distance between Rome, Pandateria and thee." The augur rolls his eyes in contempt at my corniness, but I find it uplifting, that is, as long as it is not written for all to see in some obituary. I bid the augur and the shades fair thee well, take a bow and clap my hands.

Like fragile ice, anger passes away in time.
(Ovid)

XVII

Today is the first day of spring, the morning air crisp and cool. In my second year of exile, my life is a repetitious series of unresolved grievances and ignored lamentations. "Poor Giulia", I say to myself. I relive the same old stories over and over again, like poor Sisyphus rolling the stone up the hill, only to watch it descend to the bottom, then with resolute determination repeating the process over and over, not recognizing the futility of it all. I myself do recognize the futility, but it does not seem to hinder this descent into the dark shroud of despair.

Today, I recalled two dreams from the time when my life as I knew it came to an abrupt end. The dream was so perplexing that even one as adept at interpretation as Lucretius or any of the other augurs might have had trouble explaining parts of it. The late, but not forgotten Cicero who held that dreams were nothing more than superstition and stifled our intellectual energies would have scoffed at my urgent need to take this important dream to the augur. But my freedom to come and go had come to an end, so I was left to my own devices, which are sorely wanting. In the end, once I told Livia about the dream, she sent the augur to me.

In the first dream from not so long ago, I was dressed in un-dyed and tattered sackcloth with worn ragged strips dangling like shriveled leaves about to fall. How obvious can a dream get? Still, at the time, I was bewildered.

In my mind I imagine the augur speaking of impoverished souls and shoddy morality. I recognized his interpretation more as a pedantic lecture, likely with a little instruction from Livia. During that time, I was enamoured with my rebellious ways, since they gave me a sense of power, over what is questionable. Perhaps therein lies the problem: I had forgotten to examine the question or I had simply been disinterested. When I dream of clothing, which I often do, most frequently it is some kind of footwear and usually not of this world.

After the augur left my imaginary conversation, I thought about some other dreams of clothing and footwear.

Once, I was adorned with sandals made of green moss, a dream I might add more suitable to Dilf's nature than my own. Another dream had me wearing exotic slippers of a waxy substance that resembled yellow orchids. These were beautiful dreams where I ambled through paradisiacal gardens. The augur once told me the dreams were portents of a journey to come and not necessarily one with a geographical destination. As always, his interpretations were revealing while at the same time concealing a hidden meaning, much like our own thoughts and feelings. I think about the many times I hid the truth from Tiberius, saying one thing while meaning another. His tirades provoked mutinous and un-wifely thoughts. Revealing them would have dire consequences. My suspicions told me that the augur had the heart of a cynic, like his teacher Cicero, and took pleasure in leaving me with more questions than answers. What kind of journey, I ask you, has no geographical destination? As usual, I pretended to understand. I nodded, but truthfully I longed to reveal my ignorance.

In the second dream, once again I am dressed in thread-bare sackcloth, but not afflicted with any grievous disease as those who wear sackcloth often are. The material was not itchy as one might expect it to be. The sackcloth covers me like a black shroud as I sit hunched cooking an egg on a grill fired by oil.

My simplified interpretation that this reflects impoverishment of spirit will have to do. My feeling is that it has to do with my situation that has left me in an unfamiliar state of slothfulness. Even though this state has been most of two years, it still does not seem familiar to me to be so tired that even getting out of bed takes enormous effort. Still, I think of this as a temporary condition. As for the dream, I do not know why I am cooking an egg and sitting on a curb like a homeless widow while picking away at the bare threads of my clothing.

So, here I am two years later, an impoverished soul reliving harms done to me by people held dear to my heart — that is, when they are not vexing my spirit. Perhaps this sorrow will subside, stifled by a yawn, for I am tired of my own whining and complaining. But there my husband is again in my mind's eye chastising and commanding me to unravel his knotted belt. As if he were here in the room with me, Tiberius demands that I come to his side to help him with the knotted belt that he cannot untangle. Fumbling with the ineptness he accuses me of, I am not able to loosen the knot. He orders me to get out of his way while ranting about my un-wifely skills, which in essence has some truth to it. I move strategically out of his way, noticing the warning signs of his bulging eyes and flushed face, signaling a soon to follow full blown tantrum accompanied by the stamping of his feet. There is something very frightening about a grown man stamping his feet.

"Do not just stand there, do something," he commanded while flailing his arms and turning in circles for want of direction. But I stood paralyzed by fear while he hurled insults, lamenting the loss of his good wife Vipsania who was removed from his side for the likes of me.

As I recall now, the eruption eventually subsided and the knot came unraveled, not unlike my husband I might add. He babbled on about my being a controlling wife and sabotaging his efforts. Then in complete exasperation, he stammered, "Get out of my way."

"Gladly," I responded, but under my breath. "What are you muttering about?" He commanded. I recall that I responded with a quickness only the cornered can muster, suggesting he calm himself, since it was not good for him to get in such a state. Then I asked if I could rub his feet, which he thankfully declined. After this episode, I had many dreams that did not require an augur for interpretation.

And so, I relived the same old story over and over again, as if I might expect to receive different results. I was never physically harmed by Tiberius, but I felt battered and bruised, his words stinging like one of Livia's slaps. When I relive his wrathful episodes I am aware of pursing my lips together, willing them into silence, while at the same time there is a yearning to scream that comes from deep inside. Even the air in the room seemed to sense his presence. Tension and anger penetrated the space. I came to dread being called to his suite.

I wonder if this is what my five years in exile will be about: reliving past hurts and injustices, cunning victories and struggles for control, slipping into my own childish ways of blubbering and living the life of a victim while begging gods and marble statues to intervene on my behalf.

I am all too aware of my own faults: they are more glaring than even Tiberius' flaws, which are many. I confess, and it does not make me feel better for it, that I used to flirt with Tiberius when we were still brother and sister, as his discomfort pleased me in a perverse sort of way. Now my shameful lust for attention and affection causes me grief and embarrassment. Strangely enough, I feel more like a harlot when I am with Tiberius than when I am with my paramours. I suppose the exile is working its magical elixir, as I do feel altered. Everything familiar has been turned upside down, and if I look in the mirror there is a sense of unfamiliarity that is disconcerting. I have no desire to spend the hours lamenting what might have been and what might come to be, and yet I do just this.

I shall resolve to refuse to be angry or embittered by the past. As Ovid would say, "anger melts like ice", or was it "anger melts like fragile ice". I shall search Augustus' library for Ovid's works. Will there be poetry in the library, I wonder? I miss poetry, for it soothes my weary soul and cocoons my body in a safe place, protecting those, like me, who are poor in spirit. "Like fragile ice, anger passes away with time". That is it, I think, but as soon as I get to thinking I am left with only uncertainties.

Early in the morning, while it is just barely light, I make my way to the dining room in search of breakfast. I am hungry. The dream of impoverishment holds some promise - why I cannot say, but it seems that this is what dreams are made of: resolutions, warnings, hope and hunger.

Damaris is surprised to see me up so early. She rolls the food cart into the kitchen as if it were routine. She scrambles some eggs, placing them on a plate with a slice of freshly made bread, some cheese and a few gooseberries still encased in their diaphanous shell. A nice cup of steaming tea completes the tray. Damaris rolls the cart to my table, and then she watches with grandmotherly attention as I eat with gusto for the first time in two years.

After satisfyingly breaking fast, I make my way to the library. On previous days this depressed me, since I had no one to teach me and no one to discuss matters that were perplexing. I avoided this room with all its academia. I note that Augustus' library is as orderly as his dress - sparse, yet adequate. It is easy to find the works of the poets and philosophers, for they all have their rightful place. I had meant to go directly to the poets, but I am distracted by thoughts on dreams and so instead pick up a volume by Aristotle.

I am aghast at the convoluted arguments and interpretations. "What in Hades' gates is he talking about?" I speak the words aloud. Then, I come upon a passage stating that dogs do not dream or could not dream because they are lowly creatures.

"But Moonbeam dreams; I have witnessed this," I tell Aristotle, as if he himself is in the room. "You are wrong about this, dare I say? There is more to life than what is in your philosophy."

Instantly, I feel chastised and recall Tiberius relating to me that the great philosopher claims that women's minds are not capable of understanding and that we are the weaker vessels. "What about Cleopatra?" I remember querying Tiberius in response.

"Cunning, perhaps," he had admitted, "but not capable like we men of deeper understanding."

"Well then, what about your mother, Livia?" I asked. Tiberius did not respond, instead he had dismissed me with a wave of his hand.

Then I come across Aristotle's characteristics of a good wife: patient, gentle, faithful, virtuous, modest, self-controlled, a slave to her husband, highly praising her husband, sharing in his adversity, adept at procreating as well as petitioning and praying to the gods. It seems I have failed miserably on all accounts, and for this I am truly feeling sorry for Tiberius that he had such a poor wife as me.

I continue reading aloud and conversing with Aristotle. I surmise from Aristotle's writings that Tiberius had failed also by not setting a good example, and that his actions have not been honourable or righteous. As for procreation, we have both failed at that. It was a miracle that I became pregnant by Tiberius and a shame that I miscarried, for our marital relations were very limited. They had come to a complete standstill when Tiberius retreated from the world that was created for him, having no interest in leadership or in our marriage.

My argument with Aristotle is now over, and my thoughts drift back to a time I felt revered by my father. He had held my cleverness and feistiness up to the young men as an example of a standard they ought to aspire to. Unfortunately, I now see it as it truthfully was: not really meaning that anything would come of this comparison, but only striving to shame the boys into being more determined in their convictions. Like the foolish young woman I was, I believed I would rule at my father's side, travel to foreign lands, converse about important matters of the state and dole out charity with a willing heart and purse. Aristotle is right: I am indeed weak in mind and in moral conviction. Furthermore, if given an important dream or warning of something ominous to come, I add so many of my own variations that it just brings confusion rather than enlightenment. I leave the library feeling defeated, perplexed and with way too many unanswered questions.

Why, I wonder, do the gods not just come out and warn us in waking life? Why do they have to use omens and dreams and wait until we are asleep to leave their convoluted messages? And last but not least, I ask, did Aristotle actually have a dog?

I lie down on the couch which would normally be used for reclining while dining, but it serves no purpose for one eating alone. I have taken to eating at the table and napping on the couch. Moonbeam lies down, curled up at my feet, as he prefers to be near but not cuddled. I cannot help but notice his dog-ness.

Tomorrow, I shall visit Ovid. He is much more sociable, entertaining and engaging. He never speaks scornfully to people and has the ability to touch the heart as well as the mind.

"It is well with my soul"
Spafford / Bliss

XVIII

"All is lost," I whisper, but this triggers a memory of the merchant staring at his empty upturned hands, uttering these same words after his wife, child and business perished in the flames. His wife had been tending to their child in the upper room. She had no means for escape as the olive oil they offered for sale fed the flames, destroying all that was precious and life-giving to him. "All is lost." I can still hear his cries.

I stare down at my own empty upturned hands that once held all things familiar. I know that my plight is not as significant as that of the poor Roman merchant, but that does not hold back my negative thoughts of real and imagined happenings. Salty tears sting my face as I name the traitors one by one, beginning as usual with Tiberius. I recollect the time I had composed a speech for him. He seemed well pleased in private, but in public I was ignored. I would not expect acknowledgment, but it would have been good to be respected. He had delivered the speech with arrogant conviction, thanking everyone except me, for his successes. Tiberius seemed to forget that our alliance was meant to bring power and prestige to our family. Mostly to him, I might add.

It seems the only time he gives mention to me is to point out some boorish or unsophisticated behaviour on my part, like the time he claimed I swept up his winnings after he won at dice. To this day, I am effectively embarrassed by my seemingly greedy behaviour, even though I cannot recall this incident in my own mind's eye. He describes the event in such vivid detail that I do not doubt the truth of his memory. It seems to me that he most often points out my shortcomings when I am looking my best and feeling confident. He has a knack for timing, particularly if I am enjoying myself. All too often, he points out how I finish my meal before he has hardly begun, or my kiss is not passionate enough, or I do not know how to spin and weave fabric appropriately, like the other wives. Actually, he is quite right about my not knowing how to be a good wife. Well, perhaps I know.

After becoming accustomed to the fact that we were bonded in marriage, I had longed for us to be a noble couple, admired and respected. Instead, we were a grave disappointment not only to Livia and Augustus, but to ourselves as well.

I suppose that people are now gossiping or delighting in my downfall, or worse yet they have totally forgotten me. Is Berenice feeding the gossip? She always delighted in hearing about my follies and gaffs, never forgetting and often reminding me, helping to keep them alive. Well, if she is fanning the flames of gossip, so be it. I am not inept at acknowledging my own shortcomings, and I am aware of how negative I have become in my thinking. I would like to remember the good times, but these are as fleeting as a memory. Some people never change. Quite likely I would not have changed either without this golden opportunity to mend my behaviour. In many ways Phoebe was a better friend, but the hidden rules of aristocracy would keep that in check.

My empty palms remind me of the time I failed to catch the fledgling eagle. When we were children, Tiberius and I climbed high on the Quirinal Hill, where Romulus ascended to heaven. There, we could watch the mother eagle and its young ones. Their nest was strategically placed into the crevice of the rock face. It was a challenging climb to the place where we hid behind the bush, quietly observing the mother eagle coming and going high above our heads. We never were able to make it to the top of the hill even though we believed in flying. It was our lucky day as the eaglets were being coaxed from their nest. It was a vision to behold as each one took their turn. The eaglets fell and fluttered, finally flapping their wings and taking flight. Some took to it more easily, catching the current and not landing with a frightening thump. Still, they were clumsy and a delight to watch. The last one was not yet ready. We could see its little head peeping over the edge of the nest. Finally, the mother coaxed it from its safe haven. It fell, fluttered feebly and fell again. I screamed, "Spread your wings! Flap your wings!" Startled, the mother eagle failed to catch the fledging with its talons. The small bird plummeted to its death. Tiberius laughed gleefully, and I cried out in pain. He laughed even harder as I stood sobbing with open inept hands.

"Now, look what you have done." Tiberius had said as he shook his head in dismay.

I wonder if this incident from long ago was a portent of the fallen woman I am today? Or was it a prediction of our stillborn baby? I place my hand over my heart as if to protect it from things gone by.

I close my empty hand into a fist.

My stomach complains, verifying Tiberius' criticism of my voracious appetite. He is quite right, once again, for even here in the depths of fiery infernos, unimaginable loss, fledgling birds, and grievous harm I am hungry and anticipating some delights that Damáris has conjured up even from our limited supplies. Damaris is a very good cook. I have learned to love her simple fare. I am not certain if I could now eat all the rich sauce and the bloodied crimson meat. I wonder if the abundance and overindulgence I used to relish might now repel me. Perhaps not, perhaps I have just forgotten. I suspect I would enjoy a platter of crisp royal purple grapes along with a bowl of cherry red pomegranate seeds, with their succulent juices dripping down my chin. My stomach growls with the thought of it all.

Along with being a good cook, more importantly, Damaris is a good person. I should like to emulate her behaviour. What I admire most is that she is slow to anger. Damaris is firm in her convictions. Her thoughtful, methodical and gentle spirit is all that I might hope to be but am most unlikely to achieve.

XIX

Watching Damaris sprinkle the oil-soaked olives with herbs reminds me of home and triggers a memory of a recent dream.

I dreamt only words: *And her place knows her no more.* There was no imagery and no allegory.

The strange dream had left me feeling desolate. It might just as well have added: "And she no longer knows who she is, having lost all that defines her."

Mentally, I make a list of the things that I am and that I am not.

I am no longer the wife of Tiberius. Likely I am no longer marriageable.

I am renounced by the person who means the most to me. I continue to be perplexed by my father's unforgiving stance.

I am no longer a part of the family. I am no longer a part of the community.

I am no longer a free person, in which case I surmise that I am a prisoner.

I am a fledgling eagle. I was not coaxed from my nest, I was pushed. At least I was given a chance, unlike poor little Aquila who did not even acquire the necessary feathers for flight.

I am impulsive and impertinent, according to Livia. I mentally cross out the 'I am' and replace it with 'I am no longer impulsive and impertinent' since there is nothing here that might make me so inclined to respond in such a way.

I am no longer witty and charming, especially without a cup or two of fine wine - clear and rich like the colour of Cleopatra's blood and Audacious' nose.

I was once a seductress and coy as a cobra, quietly choosing my prey. Now I would not know how to seduce and charm. Besides, the game is no longer intriguing and has lost its flavour. The Roman soldiers would not be satisfied with wages of salt from my cellar. If I were to lower my eyes and blink coquettishly, I would be mocked for the ridiculousness of it all.

History will deem me immoral or even refer to me as a crack-brained harlot, as my father did at the trial, if indeed there will be a record of me at all.

I am not quiet and elusive like Mishma, or responsible and fastidious like Damaris. I am not even a curiosity like Dilf. Even my servants have more flavour than I.

I am generous with alms and take satisfaction in giving gifts. But then, on the contrary, I hold on to my belongings as if they hold some inherent value. Besides, why would anyone want to part with things that bring them pleasure?

I am moody blue-grey like the dawn laden with fog. Brooding has become a fine art. I prefer it to pondering, which is too passive for me, even though I admire it in Damaris' character.

I am olive and herbs. Speaking of which, "I am hungry!"

XX

Berenice and I are shopping at the market. I walk on ahead of her down a long corridor empty of furnishings and artwork. When I reach the end I realize that Berenice is not with me. I sit down, strategically placing myself at the end of the hallway and at the top of a staircase so as not to miss her. A cloud of darkness begins to engulf me, so I make my way to another staircase leading down to the street. Then, a shroud of total darkness overwhelms me. I recall a banister on the staircase. I hurry towards it, groping and stumbling. At the bottom of the stairs someone familiar is waiting with a chariot. The driver is a stranger. They know I am lost. They will take me home. The familiar person falls asleep. The driver recklessly charges through the streets, careening around corners. People are barely able to get out of harm's way. I have to trust that the driver will take me home.

Waking from this dream, I feel relieved that I have escaped the darkness. I am audibly breathless because of the perilous ride through the streets, and I am fearful. Leaving Berenice behind has left me saddened, yet surprisingly relieved. I am filled with regret over my own impatience for not waiting for her.

Once again without the augur, I am on my own. I do the best I can, which is sorely deficient.

The darkness that had descended so quickly on me is self-explanatory. Dreaming about Berenice is not a surprise, since I have been thinking about her after receiving her unexpected letter. I think the darkness is a warning of how encompassing it can become if I do not respect its open mouth. Despondency feeds on itself, growing more ominous as time slithers on. One day is so much like the next; time has become incomprehensible. I know that lately small things have become catastrophic in my mind. I worry that I am becoming my mother's child.

The wild chariot ride reminds me of Tiberius' aggressive driving habits. He charges through the streets not caring who or what is in his way. I would not care to be in his path. More than once he has charged the stands where we sit, only to turn abruptly away at the last moment. He laughs at our fearful response. But Tiberius is familiar, and the driver is a stranger, so I suppose I have it all wrong.

I mentally list the things I have gleaned from the dream:

- A banister is like an anchor that is firm and secure.
- One staircase is ascending and the other descending. And yet the descending one is the way out. This is perplexing.
- Who or what is my banister?
- Perhaps, I am just longing for the familiar, even if the familiar casts darkness. Perhaps I ought to run from the darkness and find my own way. Just where, exactly, would I run to?
- Whom can I trust when even one's friends or family are not dependable?
- Is there anyone who has the courage to come to my rescue?

As always, this dream taxes my mind and leaves me desiring sleep to escape my torturous thoughts.

Strengthening my resolve, I refuse to succumb to its alluring ways.

Dilf – whose name means buttercup

XXI

Early in the morning, just after milking and arguing with Iscah the goat, and just after Damaris had finished with the morning breakfast cleanup, the two of us set off to the market in the town square. This is a special time for me, for I have Damaris' company all to myself. I feel guilty that I was secretly pleased that Giulia was not given permission to accompany us. On the other hand, I am selfishly happy. I can spend hours alone, comfortable with my own company, but when given the chance I can be extremely chatty. Once at the market we will go our separate ways. I will fetch our free allotment of fresh bread and Damaris will shop for eggs and vegetables.

At the baker's stall, I breathe deeply of the sweet and yeasty smell, accepting the bread with genuine gratitude. I realize they get paid for this service by the Roman government, but they provide more than just a product. The braided bread and the finishing touches attest to this.

I ask the husband and wife team tending the baker's stall if they know anything about the small island just a few miles off the coast of Pandateria. I have been curious about that place since our harrowing journey to this island. The two of them are more than happy to share their knowledge. They provided me with all the information I desired and then some. They are a harmonious couple, speaking in turns and finishing each other's sentences. My head moves from side to side, from the man to the woman, while they tell the story. In a hushed tone as if sharing a secret, the baker begins the tale.

"One dark stormy night many years ago, the gods had been on the sea for a long long time. They were sorely in need of a rest, so weary were they from their trials and tribulations."

His wife continues, "The gods spotted land, and as they drew near they noticed the cave-like grottos that lined the sea wall at the port of Pandateria. It was evident that the womb-like caves would give them shelter from the elements, and the deep rise of the cliff walls surrounding the island would give them a natural fortress of safety. Taking a liking to our beautiful island they stayed for many weeks in their new found home."

"One day a large whale, larger than any you have ever seen," continues the husband, "threatened their comfort as it spat out a huge spray of slimy sea foam from its nostrils. The frolicking whale soaked the gods right through to their skin, flooding their new home, forcing them out into the cold."

His wife continues, in a coquettish fashion. "So enamoured was the whale with its own projections of sea spray, it kept up its antics for days. A relentless rain flooded the caves, tiring the gods, especially when all they wanted was a little rest from warring, raiding, trudging through unbroken territory, and one too many violent storms."

The husband continues, "After several days of being inundated by the salty spray of the great whale, they cast lots, to deal with the frisky whale, and it fell upon Cupid. He took his quiver of arrows, and placed a lightning bolt in the bow given to him by Mars, and fired at the whale, striking his target. Immediately the whale turned to stone and became the formation you see today. Every now and then the gods return for a rest. You will know when they are here." The baker gives a nod of conviction.

His wife nods her head in ascension while I respond wide-eyed, echoing their expressions.

The baker's wife continues with a warning, "And watch for the whale when it storms, for it is then that it is allowed some freedom through the beneficence of the god Venus. Be careful not to go too near the sea, especially down by the port, as that whale could swallow up a young girl like you in one big gulp." The woman throws back her head, laughs like a horse, and bares her overly large flat teeth. Chunks of un-chewed bread cause me to turn my head away.

On the way home, I share the tale with Damaris. The two of us walk back to the villa with our produce, discussing the things that I had heard. She tells me she is impressed by my youthful wonder of the world. I can sense that Damaris is keeping some thoughts from me. She is becoming disconcerted with my constant habit of looking back over my shoulder. I try not to look back, but I am still jittery from the believable explanation of the formation of the island.

I recall the words of either the husband or the wife. I cannot remember who said what. "You will know when they are here with you." Looking back over my shoulder, once more, I imagine I hear footsteps other than our own.

I repeat the word 'benfence' over and over in my head, for it has been a while since I have added a new word to my vocabulary.

At noon, Damaris takes the bread from the market and distributes ample portions to everyone. We eat with sounds of deep appreciation. The bread is crusty on the outside, almost cutting our lips, while, at the same time, it is ever so soft on the inside. Somewhat like Iscah, I think to myself.

"There is nothing like freshly baked bread." Damaris says, "Especially when it is prepared by someone else. I would choose a thick slice of bread with freshly churned butter over a Roman feast anytime." Damaris murmurs appreciatively.

We savour the sweet and salty taste of our lunch.

Even though the evening is a time for rest, Damaris assembles all of us for a story as told by the great orator "Dilf".

I stand as tall as I can muster and relate the story with the passion it deserves, as told to me in the market, giving special emphasis to my new word - 'benfence'. The audience laughs more heartily than I anticipate, especially over the whale's antics.

After the telling of the tale, we shared our views or the origin of the island.

Giulia enjoyed the tale immensely. She claimed she saw the small island in a new light, with compassionate thoughts of the whale once being a free spirit roaming the sea. Giulia believed that she had a lot in common with that island.

Damaris shared her worries that her place of prayer might become permanently flooded.

Mishma enjoyed my animated performance. He empathized with the whale and thought he had a lot in common with that hump backed island, once being free-spirited himself.

Damaris closes the evening with a blessing, paying homage to Mishma's mother and to her own mother for this shared blessing that she discovered Mishma and she had in common. I have overheard both versions. Sometimes, the words differ, many are forgotten, some sentences are altered but the essence is the same. I came to realize that over the years the words become interconnected and meld into one as if wrapping us all in the comfort of their mothers' bosom.

"Friends, it is night. The night is for stillness. So let us be still". Damaris pauses for a moment, than continues with her soft-spoken prayer. "Let us be enfolded in quietness. It is night after a long day. What has been done has been done, and what has not been done has not been done. Let it rest. The night heralds the dawn. Let us look forward to tomorrow as a day with new possibilities. *Blessed Be.*"

Damaris' gentle voice stills and quiets our souls like a soothing balm.

Dilf – whose name means buttercup

XXII

I like the word 'exile'. It holds deep meaning. I do not mind being a party to those who are forced to live outside the camp. Damaris told me the story of Miriam. I was impressed by the loyalty of her people who would not break camp and leave without her. I understand that part of the story because I feel guilty for leaving Giulia behind while I am free to move beyond the gate. I doubt my loyalty.

I rather like it here on this quiet island where there are not so many people. I guess city life is not for me.

Giulia cries a lot — when she is not sleeping, that is. I know I should be more sympathetic to her plight, but her constant wailing and gnashing of teeth is tedious. It is not really that bad, but that is how it feels. I truly was pleased that she was not stoned to death. This is what some of the gossipers proclaimed would be a fitting punishment. That would be horrid. I cringe at the thought of it and duck as the imaginary stones strike my body. Like my mother, I mimic Giulia's sad expressions so she might then think I am sympathetic towards her. Sometimes, to help Damaris out, I comb and plait Giulia's hair. It worked for her daughter. I do it to calm her, but most of all I do it to ease Damaris' workload.

A good part of my day is spent foraging to supplement our simple diet. Sometimes, Tiberius, the custodian of our household, forgets to send Giulia's allowance or our stipends. It is then that my skills come in handy. As I pick the berries ripe for plucking, a feeling of greediness overcomes me. When I find a particularly fruitful vine, it causes me to salivate. I eat the succulent berries gustily like the Roman diners and the baker's wife who abandon their manners in favour of enjoyment. Even a cow has more restraint. I am enjoying the sensation of greed, but I am glad there is no one here to see me. Bacchus would be overjoyed by my lack of control.

We have a goat here on the island, as opposed to a cow. I need to work on this relationship. So far we are at odds, and if she is not careful I shall get out the salted wheat and wine in preparation for her sacrifice. If it were not for the cheese and the milk, I would trade this perfumed gem for the sake of some peace. All and all, I am well pleased with my lot. At this time and place I have everything I need and everything I want.

Giulia sits under the shade of a palm near the outdoor kitchen, while I clean my bounty and while Damaris prepares our meal. These are some of my favourite times, as we coax Damaris into telling us a story. Today Damaris is particularly animated and begins her story by setting the scene of Deborah, a wise prophet who sits under a palm tree handing out free advice and settling disputes. Giulia sits up straighter, and I bend my ear towards Damaris. It seems that Mishma has found some trees and shrubs nearby to prune and clear of old debris.

Damaris begins by slashing her knife through the air: "Barak, an Israelite, who is quick and sharp as a flashing sword, but is lacking in reasoning skills, which has gotten him into trouble more than once, has come to Deborah for advice. God made the earth shake, the mountains quake and the clouds pour down torrents of rain while summoning Barak to trap Sisera, the captain of a Syrian army, and defeat him before he attacked the Israelites. Barak is wont to serve God because he does not know how, and so he consults Deborah. She tells him to do battle against Sisera, and he tells her that he will not go unless she comes, too. Well then, let it be so, says Deborah, but then the victory cannot go to you. It must go to a woman. Barak eyes Deborah and thinks that if this is the way it is meant to be, so be it.

In the meantime, Sisera, who has a huge army with over 900 chariots, advances on his foe. Sisera then stops for a rest at the tent of his friend, Heber. Jael, Heber's wife, gives Sisera a lovely drink of warm goat's milk. When he is fast asleep she drives a peg right through his temple." Damaris hammers the wooden counter with her tenderizing mallet, startling the wits out of me. I hold my hand to my temple. Giulia presses her back firmly into the tree. Mishma listens attentively for the ending.

Damaris continues, "Unbeknownst to Sisera, Jael had not forgotten about her allegiance to her Israelite family. The land then flowed with milk and honey while Deborah broke out in song, singing of watering places and cunning victories, and women waiting for their loved ones to return."

Giulia and I are delighted with the story while Mishma sheds a tear and tries to restore a scalped palm to its original lustre.

It is evident by the look on Damaris' face that she is shocked and surprised by the anger she displayed when she hammered the mallet against the table, rocking it on its usual firm foundation.

Damaris later confided to me about the deep seated anger she was harbouring, and until the telling of the story, was unaware of. Damaris pondered if it was Phoebe's death, or Mishma's loss of freedom and manhood, or her own affliction that triggered her outburst. Damaris said that she preferred not to dwell on it and acknowledged that she did not have the answers. Damaris shared doubts about her faith which seemed to her was all too often filled with cunning revenge, violence and a never ending struggle for territory. Damaris wondered if humans will ever live in peace.

I listen attentively, offering no advice. This skill I have gleaned from Mishma.

Mishma — whose name means one who hears

XXIII

If I am not too tired before I fall asleep, I try to recollect stories of my family, because I am fearful of forgetting these things I hold precious in my heart. Sometimes I can conjure up only a dim image of my mother's deep brown eyes gazing tenderly on me, her treasured son. I try in vain to remember her facial features. More vivid this evening is the image of her work-worn hands mixing the injera batter, and then it seems I can actually smell the sour flatbread as it came from the fire, piping hot. I can visualize the red earthenware baker with its bottom blackened from the fire, and my mother taking off the lid to reveal the spongy treat. She would allow me to roll it flat when it was cool enough. I would poke my finger into the injera and watch as my fingerprint bounced back. My mother told me that this was the test to determine if the injera was made just right. It always was.

Just before I came to my room I passed by the kitchen. Damaris was adding some flour and water to her sour dough mixture. I realized that this aroma was the reason for my recollection. It is odd how a smell or a sound can provoke a memory when you least expect it.

I used to beg my mother, mercilessly, to tell me stories of her youth, especially the one about the hyenas. As she told it to me and as I recall, she was the second youngest of four children. All of them helped in some way to support the family. Their father, my grandfather whom I do not know, was often away on trade missions trying to provide a better living for them. In order to help with expenses, my mother Maryan would gather khat at a nearby farm. Then she would be early to market when the addicted would pay a decent price for her product. So in need were the folks to satisfy their craving that they eagerly paid a fair price, whereas later in the day with their appetite satisfied they would be more prone to bargain.

This is the story that I loved to hear as told to me by my mother: I can still hear the quiver of fear in her voice recounting the episode.

One day as I walked to market with a cache of khat slung over my shoulder, I had an eerie feeling of being watched. I glanced sideways and caught a glimpse of skillful predators, pacing methodically. They had a recognizable sideways gait. The profile of their high shoulders along with their massive heads told me that they were not dogs but, unmistakably, hyenas. I stole myself to keep walking, more quickly now and without as much as a sidelong glance, for I knew if I saw their eyes or their sharp teeth I would freeze with fear. First, I quickened my gait and then I broke into a full run, heading as fast as possible to the guava tree. I scurried up that tree, just in time for I sensed them nipping at my heels. The two hyenas paced back and forth, round and round, clawing at the tree, drooling, while their powerful jaws clicked with anticipation. I clung to the tree with an iron grip, keeping my feet tucked into an uncomfortable position, barely out of reach of the hungry, menacing hyenas.

It seemed to take forever for the sun to rise and for the rooster to crow in a new day. I hoped it would not be my last. I searched the horizon for anyone, perhaps a nearby farmer on the way to market. The only sounds were of my own heavy breathing and the cackling barks of the hyenas below. With every ounce of courage I could muster, I did not shift my position. My foot was now numb and tingling, I was in desperate need of some respite. My hands began to shake uncontrollably. Fortunately, this loosened a guava which fell to the ground, startling the hyenas. Meanwhile, there was another commotion down the road. This further disruption caused the hyenas to retreat, reluctantly. I loosened my grip and began hurling guavas at my predators. My accuracy surprised even me. I would like to say that after abandoning their prey they disappeared from view and from my mind. But the truth is their yellowed eyes and frothing mouths haunted me for some time.

The herdsman waving his shepherd's hook came running towards the tree. Trailing close behind him was my younger sister Khadja, crying rather incoherently, but pointing in the right direction. Snuffing off my heartfelt gratitude, as if his rescuing me were nothing more than part of his day's routine, the herdsman walked with us towards town. He kept us company until we reached our home. I hid under the covers for the rest of the day.

Fortune would have it that my routine was to stop and collect Khadja who would then go to market with me, after I had gathered the khat. I was late that day. Khadja became concerned and came looking for me. The nearby herdsman was another stroke of good fortune. I shiver with fear to think of what might have happened to her had he not come along.

Khadja took the khat to market and held out for a very good price. I was ever so proud of my little sister.

I never tired of hearing about my mother's harrowing adventure. When my mother did not care to recite this story to me, once again, for I could be a pest, she would tell me of the land that my father came from. He told her that there was a forest nearby with eucalyptus trees that made breathing easy. Further to the east were rock formations. The stones and the rocks created their own works of art that resembled imaginary creatures more frightening than hyenas. My mother smiled when she spoke of my father's teasing ways. She told me he would growl with emphasis, while at the same time reassuring her with a tender caress.

Maryan, my mother, met Mesfin, my father, who was from the northern part of Ethiopia. My father had come to the Upper Nile region when on a trade mission. He said that once he met my mother he never looked back. My father was a learned man, able to read and keep accounts. He taught me these skills when he had time. I am afraid they are becoming weak with misuse, like muscles. My mother used to tell me that I looked like my father and then kindly describe how handsome he was, causing me to lower my eyes to hide my pride. Although she never spoke the words aloud, I knew that I was precious in her eyes.

I recall that the rocks and soil where our family lived were a deep reddish colour. I remember that our family lived in the countryside, which was marked with bean and guava trees: the kind that helped the traveler with direction, the kind that were heavy with fruit, the kind that could survive, and the kind that saved my mother's life.

XXIV

Tiberius has died and I feel no remorse.

I awake from the dream feeling desolate, because I am so lacking in compassion. To make amends for my callousness, I decide to list Tiberius' positive traits, as an honourable widow might be so inclined to do. There is a reality to the feelings in this dream that is thought provoking.

I sit in blank silence.

My attention turns to the rhythmic slap of the waves against the shore. I watch as the light nymphs dance across the surface of the sea, bedazzling the dark azure blue and turning it into sun-kissed turquoise gems. The nymphs coax me to go beneath its surface beauty to the mystery that lies below. I imagine wrecked ships, rotting cargo, skeletal remains, menacing predators, cornered victims, stones, rocks; maybe even mountains, but likely only caverns. There is a muffled silence down here on the plateau at the prow of the island, like when you put your ear to a sea-shell.

The morning sun beats down. Perspiration runs down my forehead and into my eyes. I speculate for reasons why the sea never loses its flavour. I wonder where the salt comes from. Are there salt mines down there or does it come from land near the sea, like Ostia where Dilf comes from? Either way it is assaulting my eyes with its acerbic wit. The more I rub them the more irritated they become.

The morning has disappeared, along with the dancing nymphs. I arise and stumble. Watching the waves for too long has made me dizzy. My stomach is also queasy, refusing to rise and swell in synchronicity with the sea. I have spent too much time watching wave after wave. It has broken my concentration into little bits of inert sand with no trace whatsoever of Tiberius' good traits.

After a light lunch of figs, goat cheese and one too many slices of Damaris' bread, I sit for a while in the shade of the arbour by the pool. I drop a pebble into the water and watch as it ripples from the centre, moving outward and getting progressively larger. I think perhaps that Tiberius is at his darkest when he is nearest the centre of Roman life, needing to distance himself from all the obligations that he has no taste for. I accept the fact that our marriage belongs to that dark centre. As the circle moves outward, the edge becomes more irregular and then disappears. He is, indeed, irregular. "Is that a positive trait?" I doubt my ability to stay focussed on the task at hand. I drop another pebble.

Organized! Tiberius has organization skills. He is thrifty, and generous, but only with outside funding. He is good looking. "No," I chastise myself. That is not a trait. He has a talent for learning Greek and Latin. And he is learned when it comes to mythology. Actually, he is pedantic, which cancels out the attribute.

Personally, what I liked best about Tiberius were his long absences.

I hope to drop off into a dreamless nap. When I awake, I will be refreshed and able to live two days in one, just like Damaris proclaims.

XXV

Narcissus would be proud of me, so obsessed am I with my own predicament. I am thinking that the reason for all the calamities in my life is my neglect of the gods. It is true: I have turned my back on them. They echo my sentiments.

I am willing to reconsider and give them an opportunity to redeem themselves.

Just for good measure, I will also pay homage to Romulus and Remus, the founding fathers of Rome. I wonder whether the lives of my family would have been different if Romulus had not killed Remus. We seem to be plagued by one disaster after another. The death of my husband Marcellus affected both me and my father Augustus. Marcellus was favoured by my father, which in turn helped to keep me in favour. There is an equestrian statue of Marcellus at the market square that depicts him as a military hero. His muscular breasts are evident even beneath the bronze breast plate. My memory of him seems to be more of this statue than that of the real man. He brought out what was best in me. This was no easy task.

Thinking about Romulus and Remus and their father who was sent into exile somehow seems to placate me. I guess it is soothing somehow to know you are not alone in your circumstance.

This is their story as told to me by my father.

Two brothers inherited the kingdom of Alba when their father died. Numitor became king. He was a good ruler, wise and loved by his people. Amulius retired at an early age after completing his education. Amulius lived in luxury contemplating his riches, counting his money, and admiring his treasures, while his eyes grew more bulbous with each acquisition. Soon enough, he became bored with his idle life and conquered Alba, defeating his brother Numitor. He sent Numitor into exile on a farm near the Tiber River. He imprisoned Numitor's pregnant daughter. Numitor did not understand how his daughter became pregnant, because she was virtuous and not betrothed to anyone. He was told by a seer that she was impregnated by the god Mars. This placated him, somewhat. Still, he worried about what the neighbours might think.

Numitor's daughter, Artesia, gave birth to twin boys. Amulius told his slave to throw them in the river. The slave took the babies to the river but did not have the heart to follow the orders to drown them. Instead he made a reed basket and lined it with pitch. Then he placed the twins in the basket and gently pushed them out onto the current which carried them away.

The basket containing the twins, eventually, drifted onto shore. The twins landed by a beautiful grove rich with plants, fruit trees and all kinds of things pleasing to the eye. The river watered the paradisiacal garden. Animals came to this place to drink and to graze. Fortunately for the boys, a she-wolf who had recently lost her cubs heard the babies cry and came to see what all the fuss was about. The wolf felt sorry for the hungry babies and suckled them. Overhead and high above an eagle viewed the scene. It also took pity on the babies and fed the twins seeds, worms, plants and all things pleasing to the palate.

One day a herdsman came leading his flocks to the grove to graze and to drink from the sweet water. He found the babies and took them home to his wife. She nourished and cherished them, naming them Romulus and Remus. The twins flourished, becoming wise and strong.

The curious boys soon found Numitor's farm, which was nearby. They got caught in the middle of a skirmish with some other troublesome boys. All of them were brought to Numitor to explain their actions. As Numitor heard their story from the beginning and to the present, he realized that the twin boys were his grandsons.

Numitor told the boys that their mother Artesia was still imprisoned and that their Uncle Amulius had conquered Alba from him. Romulus and Remus formed a small army of disgruntled people. This was easy to do since the king was not good to his people, overtaxing them and spending the money flagrantly. The kingdom was defeated, and Romulus' and Remus' mother was freed from prison, while their Uncle Amulius was thrown into the river with stones tied to his ankles for good measure.

Artesia begged Romulus and Remus to stay, but they had their own plans to build a city by the banks of the River Tiber where the she-wolf and the eagle had fed them.

Remus wanted to build their city on the Aventine Hill, while Romulus wanted to build on the Palatine Hill. They had a scuffle. Remus fell down hitting his head on a stone and died.

Romulus buried his brother between the two hills. He placed samplings of the best crops into his grave so that the city would prosper. He marked the site with a sculpture of a wolf with an eagle on its back and two male babies sucking the wolf's teats.

As I recount the story in my mind, I am amazed how some things never change. Just recently, as Scribonia informed me, my father purged the Senate of unscrupulous members who were using the public funds in personal ways that could not be overlooked. Still, after all these years, there are those who use unethical methods to enhance their lives and those who dedicate their lives to improving society. Unfortunately, I fit both molds and have discovered all too late that I would like to be chosen as one who serves humankind. I squirm at the thought of this unlikely result. I have wasted many years in fruitless pursuit of false values. I am more like the Senators than I would like to admit. My choices were poor ones. Perhaps if given another chance I could at least improve someone's lot in life.

Now I am left with a dilemma. How might I pay homage to Romulus and Remus without a craftsman or a poet? My mind is dull from misuse.

I thought about composing a poem with intricately woven silken words, but I do not have the imagination to think up even one stanza. Furthermore, I will not resort to being a rhyme master.

My thoughts turn to a visual image. I might sculpt an image of a she-wolf nourishing the twin boys, but that has already been sculpted and bronzed by someone more accomplished than I. Perhaps I will weave two pieces of cloth together into a rope, but then what? I might entwine a honeysuckle vine throughout the rope. As the bell-like flowers grow in pairs, the meaning would be rich in symbolism, but visually I do not think it would be too exciting. It would require time and patience; on the other hand, I cannot foresee time being a problem.

Rome was built on seven hills, I think to myself, imagining the hills forming out of a volcanic explosion. Then there are the twins to consider.

Yes, that is it! I exclaim out loud. I will get Mishma to bring me some of the soft volcanic tuft from the harbour. The project will require a considerable amount of material. I will sculpt seven hills with my own hands. Honeysuckle will be planted in the valleys. The vines will meander here and there, throughout the hills. The flowers will blossom in pairs. Like an aspen grove that has many trees but only one root system, it will symbolize our family's shared history. Eventually, the vines will climb upwards towards our common goal of the *Pax Romana*. It will be placed in the garden surrounding the central pool and become a part of the landscape.

Anticipating the final result fills me with joy. I will have to acquire the virtue of patience, but I shall not let this dampen my enthusiasm.

I examine my soft hands and wonder why I have never thought to put them to use. Of course, they have always been a work of art in themselves, adorned with splendid jewels and silky smooth in their texture. Worried now about the damage I might incur, I will ask Dilf to make me a clay mask for my hands to restore them to their original lustre. For now, I am quite excited and cannot wait for Mishma to bring me the material.

Dilf - whose name means buttercup

Salary n. a fixed compensation paid periodically to a person for regular work or service
Origin - salt for wages

XXVI

"You are worth your salt, Dilf." Damaris hands me my salary. I gather my father's debt must be paid in full. With tears of overwhelming pride, I stand up straight and accept this first payment for services rendered. I am handed a cake of salt pressed with an image of our emperor, Caesar Augustus, along with some coins. My thoughts turn to the benefits of salt. This is a portion of my wages and as good as a coin. Salt is sometimes used to pay soldiers and servants. It is used to preserve food and enhance flavour. It can be used at the market to barter for goods. Without salt we would be in a quandary. I am worth my salt. That is my worth. I am incorrigibly proud.

"I will need a bowl for these salty tears," I tell Damaris.

I am overwhelmed by all this unexpected extravagance. I have never had a coin of my own before. Now, I stare at a handful. I muster a blubbery thank you and run to my room, where I hold the coins close to my heart and reflect on this first payment. I cannot keep from weeping, as I wonder what I will do with my salary. I have never had to deal with such an ominous task before. Maybe I will preserve one of the coins, for it holds greater meaning than anything that I might buy with it. I place a denarius coin carefully and tenderly in my brown earthenware jug, sprinkling it with a dash of salt from a corner of my measure. This is more than just money: it speaks to me of independence and wealth beyond one's comprehension, and pride in one's work and self-worth and unimaginable affirmations. I look in the jug to see if it is still there. There it is, preserved in salt, just like Lot's Wife, who now stands petrified as a salt pillar overlooking the Dead Sea for all to see.

Damaris told us the story of Lot's wife and how she was a 'pillar' in her community. She was so concerned for those she had left behind, she forgot God's commandment and looked back to see if her relatives and friends had escaped the burning town of Sodom. The towns of Sodom and Gomorrah were being razed because of the citizens' licentious behaviour. I suppose Damaris told this story to give some hope to Giulia that her character might be preserved. Lot's wife was instantly transformed into a pillar of salt with her body turned towards the town of Sodom and her eyes transfixed on her loved ones. I imagine that light from the sun reflects off the mineral deposits, bounces off her statue bedazzling those who gaze upon her. I shall give her a name of her own and call her Scintilla.

Now I carry Damaris' words into the rest of the day. Today is a new day, and I am worth my salt. I hold my head high and straighten my shoulders. I stand tall like a pillar.

Yesterday I spotted some mushrooms, and now I am going to go and pick the best ones. I marked the place with a red cord so I can easily locate them. If I have time, I will try and find some hazelnuts, too.

This has been a very good day in my life, one of the best ever.

Damaris – whose name means heifer

XXVII

Giulia had not yet recovered from the shock of the death of her first born son, Gaius, in a battle at Lycia when she received word of the death of her second born son, Lucius, in Massilia. Both young men were killed on the front lines, which is not a position one would expect them to be in. It was an honour, Livia stated in her letter.

Some honour! That is all I have to say.

What can one say that might bring comfort when one is rendered speechless?

We all react differently to grief. Giulia cannot verbalize her sorrow which measures deeper than the infinite ocean. It seems as if her life blood has ceased to flow, petrified like the veins in our marbled paradise.

Mishma prunes the shrubs to within a hare's breadth of their lives. He yanks out weeds with a vengeful fury. He takes his anger out on his tools, banging and clanging the instruments that he usually treats with tender and prideful care.

I do not believe Dilf is grieving, but she closes her eyes as if in sorrow and speaks in hushed tones.

As for myself, I have an urge to help everyone. I bring them water and prepare food. I would do this anyway, but now it carries special meaning. I have trouble concentrating, forgetting what I have mixed into the batter or worrying about what I have left out. I barely have the stamina to make it through the daily chores. There is a heaviness in my legs that feels like I have been shackled. I cannot imagine the impact the black gall plays on Giulia's body. Despair seems to be her only companion. I weep buckets of tears for Giulia and for myself, as hers have turned to chalk.

If I ask her what I can do to help, she opens her mouth like a newborn chick, but no sound comes out.

I lay my burdens down at the altar of my cave. I pray in silence, for I am at a loss for words. The silence answers my call. I will approach the others. We will have a funeral. It cannot be a traditional Roman funeral with chanters and processions. One of us will eulogize the boys. Women are not allowed to eulogize, so that leaves Mishma. I will ask him if he will honour the boys. We will all help him with this important task. I will trust that this is the right thing to do. It will break open our hearts. Perhaps the rending will help in some small way.

We will not require professional mourners.

XXVIII

Damaris, a servant of the Roman Empire

To Livia, counsellor of Rome

We your servants continue to be grateful for the privilege of serving Rome.

We have hired a woman from the village who is instructing Giulia on weaving and spooling. It is evident that Giulia has taken to her lessons with a zeal you would admire. Her adeptness on the loom impresses us.

We are pleased to send you this good news.

Greetings from all of us.

Agitated once again with the responsibility of reporting on Giulia's progress, I take it out on the laundering.

No one would likely be able to understand the severity of Giulia's punishment, I muse to myself as I scrub the wet clothing up and down the washboard. Some might assume that it would be a blessing to be removed from family or to be alone on a remote island. Let me assure you, it is a trial to be so isolated. Even the three of us servants, who have good reason to be wary of humankind, feel quite alone. We look forward, with the zeal of an expectant mother, to market day, the second Tuesday of each month. Wiping the perspiration from my brow, I realize I cannot dwell on leaving Giulia behind while the rest of us are free to come and go.

As the wet clothing becomes immersed in the water, it becomes heavier and difficult to turn. The spasm in my back is a reminder to be careful. I deeply regret asking Livia for permission to take Giulia to the market. I wring out the neck of the shift, squeezing it with all my might.

The only other respite I have is on Monday evenings when I zigzag my way down to the port to the grotto cave. I have turned it into a haven for solitude and prayer. This cave is of no use to the shore-men since Jonah's path gets swallowed up when the tide comes in. The first part of my evening compline is spent in silent prayer. Then I recite a scripture from memory. Even though it is likely not word for word, and even though I know it is against the law for women to be reflecting on such matters, I talk to God about the words that resonate with me and of course the things that are troubling. Then the prayer time is completed with murmurings for only God to hear.

I have an altar with the crystal retrieved from the cave beneath our home in Greece, and a candle to light the darkness in this place that has been molded by the wild sea. When I light the candle there is an eerie glow revealing dancing shapes on the wall, bobbing about like a covey of partridges. On this altar, there is also a seashell broken open to reveal five tiny perfect white doves. I was so distraught when the shell broke in two, but then this miracle showed itself as a sign from God. This is the mystery of faith. Belief is all that is required from me.

The cave smells of musty moss. The sound of the sea is barely audible. When I put a conch shell up to my ear, it reminds me of the sounds of this house of prayer. Part of the scripture that I remember says that God knows everything about me, even from the time that I was knit together in the womb of my mother. This cave puts me in that dark, moist and protective space. This wild, yet peaceful, place brings me solace.

When the ground beneath my feet becomes damp and cold, it is a sign for me to leave. Also, it is a reminder that there is more to be soaked than my feet. The olives are waiting.

XXIX

My last coherent memory was of Mishma carrying me to the villa. There is a span of time missing between then and now. During that lapse, I swam in churning waters. When I was not drowning, I walked on flat land and gazed at a flat sky. Clouds rolled in and clouds rolled out. Tides came in and tides receded. The sun rose and the sun set. I heard bitter howls from the bowels of the earth. Then there was silence. Everyone, so it seemed, turned a deaf ear to my cries. I stared at the world around me, but there was nothing to see.

Today, for no inexplicable reason, the cloud ceiling lifted.

My movements are cautious for fear of returning to that place of darkness. I breathe deeply of the freshness of this new day. The window allows a beam of light to enter my room. My gaze rests on the rays filtering through the silk curtain like a veil of gossamer. I survey the rest of the room. It looks different somehow – brighter, perhaps. No, more peaceful.

Dilf sits nearby and sees me stirring. She jumps from her chair calling urgently for Damaris.

Her excitement affirms that I am not dreaming.

In my imagination, I hear a trumpet heralding a new day. Even if I am hearing things that are not of this world, I am not deterred. It is good to feel a spark of vitality. It is good to feel anything.

XXX

March of our 3rd year has passed, but today is still in keeping with the bone-chilling damp weather of the past few months. Nevertheless, it helps to pass the day if I visit the sea. I am finished with brooding, pleading and venting my anger, since it has not made a difference to my predicament. But loneliness clings to me like a slug sucking the blood from my heart. Exile is my faithful companion. There is nothing I can do to avoid it.

The waves sing their dirge as if I were amongst the dead. I do not stay long today, since my body is tense like a loom from this incorrigible weather. Furthermore, I refuse to listen to its lament.

Sarcastically I tell myself that now that I have finished with the cheerful part of my day, I will go back to the villa for my second weaving lesson. Damaris has made arrangements with a wonderful woman from the village named Dorcas. She looks like an aged gazelle with long spindly legs and graceful movements, especially when she is weaving on the loom. Even when she is spooling, her adeptness is mesmerizing.

Her first words capture my attention: "The first weave of the shuttle is called the sacred weft." Dorcas continues, succinctly, but with clarity, on how to get the tension in the first row just right.

"From then on everything will go more smoothly," she tells me.

"The weft is the thread you use to weave through the lengthwise threads of the warp." She looks up to see if I am listening. I nod like an obedient pupil. Indeed, I am attentive, for once because I am interested in learning. Dorcas has the patience of Sarah, a woman Damaris told me about who had to wait until she was 90 years old to get pregnant with her first child. Apparently, she laughed out loud. Some joke! Thoughts mingle with thread, and I reminisce over a time back in Rome when I never took to working wool. I had better things to do and no patience for this work. But the weaver-woman captivates me with her intensity. I find myself being most attentive to the instructions and not to regrets of the past. It seems to me that my life would have been very different if I had learned to pay attention to the first weave of the shuttle. Our hour together passes swiftly.

After she leaves, I spend another hour or so practising. I look forward to her return. She is a very good teacher, even though she is a woman of few words.

Old habits are hard to break. I find myself back in Rome, and wondering what if I had a mentor like Dorcas to teach me about life. I might have made someone a good wife. On second thought, maybe not! What if I had been allowed to marry Antonius instead of Tiberius? What if Antonius were allowed to speak on our behalf? What could he have possibly said that might have made a difference? Would he have told of our aspirations to succeed my father? We likely would have been crucified for treason. That is more likely the outcome.

It is best not to think of what became of Antonius. He was not my first suitor to disappear. I never considered what happened to the other unsuitable candidates. Likely banned, I once thought, now I am not so sure.

I am aware that I can be naïve, especially when it comes to flattery. I know full well that some used me to advance their position. Well so be it, I also used them to satisfy my need for affection and attention. What if Antonius had been using me for his own gain? That is a thought I ought to perish. I hope not, for I did care for him. He was not like the others. His feelings for me felt authentic. Besides, he was ever so pleasing to look at. He had the physique of an athlete with good definition in all the right places.

Today was a reasonably good day. I would like to leave it that way, so I leave Rome to its own problems.

My back speaks more eloquently than words. It is time to quit. Besides, I need more wool, and so far I have not been taught to love spinning.

The next morning I am back at my usual perch, staring out to sea. I think I see a ship, but I have been tricked before by Old Proteus, who delights in my gullibility with his tempting mirages. I dare not hope, not wanting to have it dashed against the rocks like the incessant waves crashing, crashing, and crashing over and over again. The sea is not satisfied until it puts me back in a dark mood. 'Misery loves company'. I jut my chin out in defiance and flail my arms mimicking the wave's absurd behaviour.

The image of a ship looms larger. I have lost my resolve and immerse myself in hope. Perhaps it will bring a visit by my mother, some badly needed supplies, not to mention my allowance, the servant's wages and some news. I long for news of Rome. After a long winter, we are low on everything except fish and olive oil. There are only so many things Damaris can do with fish and olive oil.

The sun is high in the sky. The haze has lifted, allowing a clear view. Even in my anxious state, I could not help enjoy the beauty of the sun challenging the mist.

I squint so I can see more clearly. There is no question now. It is indeed a ship. I ask the sea , " is my mother on the ship? What news will she bring?" As usual, I receive no reply. My heart pounds heavily against my chest, making it difficult to rush back to the villa to tell the others. They will be just as excited as I am. Any variation to our mundane existence brings great joy.

The four of us give up on our routine even though we know it will take hours before the ship is docked and the cargo is unloaded. We are unable to focus on our daily tasks. I ask the guard to open the gate and let Damaris, Dilf and Mishma go down to the dock. He usually makes me distance myself, but today he exhibits a show of humanity and opens the gate wide for the three of them. You can tell that he is also anxious, since his trembling hands fumble with the lock. After they leave, the key in the lock turns. The familiar sound of grating metal on metal followed by a sharp clink, signals my seclusion from the rest of the world. With his back turned to me, the gate-keeper has returned to his rigid position.

While I wait, I pace, I sit, then pace again. The hours pass ever so slowly. I shake like a leaf on a quivering aspen.

I laugh joyfully at the sound of my mother's voice shouting orders left and right. The anxiety of the weary traveler is evident in the shrillness of her voice. I breathe a sigh of relief knowing that none of this is a dream. You would think my tears would have dried up by now, but they flow with reckless abandon, like a giddy gambler gleaning his winnings.

The supplies are bountiful. The workers shuttle back and forth loading and unloading keg after keg and amphora after amphora. A child sits high atop a pile of sacks. How strange a sight! Seldom do you see a workman with a child. His wife must be very ill, or some such calamity must have befallen him. He lifts the child down and hands her over to Scribonia. I am perplexed. This is not like my mother to take a waif under her wing. The child is scrawny and yellowish in colour, with very large eyes. It is plain to see, she will soon give up the ghost.

Scribonia pours out the details like a broken sack of wheat spilling out its contents, all the while hurling orders at all of us: "This is Claudia, your granddaughter. Giulia the Younger is dead. What shall I do with this child? She cannot go back to Rome. Giulia the Younger was banned for life. I was made to go visit her. We took supplies. It was too late. Here, take her. I wash my hands of this whole business. I need to lie down."

Scribonia continues railing against the injustices that have befallen her while in the same breath directing her commandments toward Damaris, Dilf and Mishma. Everyone scurries to help: Mishma giving direction for the supplies, Damaris almost carrying Scribonia and Dilf running for water. I am left staring in disbelief at this emaciated child. Her eyes appear too big for her head. Her bony frame reveals her dreadful state. How does this happen? I am incensed! My father prides himself in the fact that no Roman shall go hungry, and yet here is living proof that this is not always the case. I carry the child to the kitchen and get her a cup of goat`s milk. Dilf catches me just in time taking the cup from my hand, warming the milk and diluting it with water. She tells me to make sure the child sips it slowly. Dilf scurries to warm a blanket by the oven for Scribonia. I tend to the child. She sips disinterestedly but takes it all in. She does not speak. I lie her down on my bed and wrap the blanket snuggly around her gaunt frame.

The child sleeps. Scribonia sleeps. I stare in disbelief at the upheaval of our usually tidy home. More and more, I have come to appreciate my father's penchant for orderliness.

Did Scribonia actually say that my daughter was dead? This little bit of news was dropped as if it were scraps for the dogs. Has yet another of my children died? How can one person lose three children in such a short time? What are the gods up to now? Who have I offended? All this retribution is simply unfathomable. I lower my eyes in shame, as if I am somehow responsible.

I know in my heart and in my mind that it would not have been possible for Giulia the Younger to cope with exile. She was always so high strung, always on edge, and needing to be placated. I am afraid my daughter was not pleasant to be with. I clasp my hand over my mouth at the horror of thinking a bad thought about the dead. I am so sorry my poor girl had to die to find some peace. The *Pax Romana* has a voracious appetite.

Feeling very tired, helpless and confused by the day's events, I lie down beside the child and fall into a fitful sleep. When I awake, I feel dumb like a petrified log, but the child in the crook of my arms is ever so real. "Claudia", I say her name aloud and tell myself that the child has a name.

Naming her gives a realization that this is my grandchild. This little girl was three years old when I left Rome. This wisp of a thing does not in any way resemble that child. I recall that the child was very conscious of herself, even at such a young age becoming easily embarrassed over trivial matters. I smile when I think of the memory of her holding her breath and turning blue when her mother wrestled her doll from her arms. Claudia clung to that doll with its threadbare clothing like her life depended on their connectedness. We had to douse her with water to force her breath. There is no evidence of that strong will in this broken spirit.

The memory of Claudia clinging to that doll has provoked thoughts of grief and how it hangs on with the same determination. Grief is cruel and takes pleasure in striking out at the already helpless. There is nothing one can do to make it disappear. I have but one child left, and I am helpless and confused by it all. I reach out and shake my fist as if to break down the gate of this abysmal prison. Grief's salty sea slaps me hard in the face. It has won the day after all.

XXXI

Dilf likely does not have a cure for neglect, but if she has anything to do with it, the child will survive.

I am reticent to claim her, for I fear it will only bring disaster upon her. On the other hand, the child fills me with hope. My emotions are having a tug of war pushing and pulling, gaining then losing ground. If only I could do it all over again, I would try to get it right. I wish I had been a better mother to my children, more practical like Dilf, more nurturing like Damaris and more attentive like Mishma. I would not scold like my mother Scribonia is prone to do. On the other hand, at least she pays attention to me. My mother starts a lot of sentences with 'you should' or 'you ought to'. Admittedly, it provokes me into a state of defiance, every time I hear those words. But then I excuse her and admit that mothering was not one of my strong suits either.

I have found mothering to be confusing. First of all, there are other's expectations which were not in keeping with my own. Feeling inadequate, I would then make more of an effort. I was so easily sidetracked with things that interested me more, such as fashion, festivities and all things that I now consider frivolous. I am now grateful that these distractions have lost their lustre. I rather enjoyed my children when they were babies. I can still feel their little beating hearts next to mine. They trusted me, perhaps the only people who ever did. I did not care for tantrums and wailing, and snotty noses made me gag.

I guess I was more compassionate than I give myself credit for. It broke my heart to lose that baby not yet ready to come out of the womb. No first cry, no beating heart, just so still and so small. I do not care to think about it.

The boys were taken from me at an early age to be conditioned in the men's court for their important roles in the empire. Truthfully, I was not capable of dealing with their exuberance. It was better to have brief visits with them.

Agrippina and Giulia the Younger stayed in the women's court to be raised by the women. Thinking about it now and realizing how limited our time together was, if I could change things, I would like to have spent more time with them. Instead, I devised ways to shirk my motherly duties.

I liked being pregnant, because then I could have lovers without fear of our lineage being tainted. When I told my father this, he laughed heartily. We sometimes shared intimate details of our erotic adventures. The sharing of our adventures came to an end when he became smitten with Livia.

For now, I cherish every moment I spent with all five of my children, and wish I had more memories. The things I took for granted are now treasured in my heart.

I shake off these memories of how things ought to have been and focus on this day. How wonderful it is to have Scribonia, the child, and Dilf to dine with. I do not believe I ever dined alone until I came to this island.

Cheese, olives, pickled herring, dried grapes and Damaris' sourdough bread are laid out on the table. I have become used to our plain fare and rather enjoy it. It is not to Scribonia's liking, and she lets it be known. She resents the fact that Dilf reclines at Claudia's side. I insist on it, since she is nursing the child back to health slowly and with conviction. For now, she feeds her small portions, to which Scribonia also takes exception. I would prefer to see her eat more, but I trust in Dilf's nurturing ways.

Scribonia monopolizes the conversation with news that I was recently longing to hear but now leaves me disinterested, for I am still trying to come to terms with the death of Giulia the Younger.

Scribonia begins salting her news with her own views:

- Berenice is betrothed to King Archelaus. Imagine that! She might become a queen! I have a letter for you, from her, in my baggage. I will give it to you later.

- A peace fountain was built in front of the Pantheon at huge expense, costing as much as a legion's wages, they say. Spectacular displays of water cascade out of four mouths. The fountain in all its splendour is meant to represent four symbols of the *Pax Romana*: a white dove for peace, a gavel for justice for all, a mask for culture and the arts, and an arch of course for Roman innovation in architecture. Your father is certainly obsessed with arches. I admit, these solid structures that dominate the landscape do have a tendency to glorify Imperial Rule.

- Now that we are a peace-keeping nation, your father is being depicted in monuments as "The Prince of Peace" rather than a "Roman Military Hero". He is certainly astute when it comes to propaganda.

My thoughts turn to the Pantheon that my husband Marcus Agrippa built. One had a sense of tranquility when entering, which he told me was achieved through balance and proportion. I recall looking upwards and being bedazzled by a magnificent dome all covered in bronze tiles, with an opening in the centre to reveal the heavens. My husband was brilliant. Yes, he was, I nod in affirmation of this memory. Scribonia smiles thinking I am responding to her news. He would have been devastated by the deaths of Lucius and Gaius. It is almost a relief that he did not live to rue these dark days. I think he must have built that golden portal to the heavens unknowingly for our boys to pass through.

Scribonia continues on, barely taking a breath, energized by the news she has to offer and a captive audience at her disposal.

- Yet another new library has been built.

  I wonder if there are enough books and scrolls for all those buildings.

- More bridges. I am certain it is to accommodate your father's need for more arches. Just how many arches can an eye behold?

- My mother does not wait for a reply and continues on without taking a breath.

- Rome is growing so fast. I do not like it. All that traffic. Everything and everyone moves so fast. There are too many people, too much noise and it is too busy for me. It is quiet here — too quiet for my liking.

- The Senate has been purged. This is the big news. There are too many embarrassing mishaps. They forgot to be discreet with their spending. They claimed the same expense in different ways. It is difficult to comprehend. Imagine! They are paid such an exorbitant salary to begin with. Probably nothing would have been done except for a slap on the wrist, but the plebeians rebelled and withheld taxes. As you well know, public scorn embarrasses your father. Augustus was truly angered by Lucius Paulus and the senator's ostentatious displays of luxury and lavish spending.

- The Tiber River is being cleaned of all the rubble. People just rid themselves of their waste, expecting it all to sink to the bottom. I suppose they think the river will swallow the revolutionaries without repercussions, like Cronus devoured his children. Soon enough, too much debris floated to the top. The river and its shoreline are disgusting.

In a hushed tone as if she were in a crowded room and might be overheard, Scribonia whispers that in his old age my father has taken to gambling too much and, not only that, on a working day.

I open my mouth to speak, but it is too late. Scribonia hardly takes a breath and continues on.

- A new coin has been cast with the image of Capricorn and the star that Augustus was born under. I brought you some. Remind me to give them to you later.

"Would you kindly tell me about my daughter?" I ask in a voice more impatient then I had intended.

"Of course, I was saving that for last to give it the importance it deserves." Scribonia straightens her back in indignation at the tone of my voice.

"As you already know, Giulia the Younger and Claudia were exiled shortly after your own banishment. But you likely did not know all the details that came out afterwards. After Lucius Paulus' disappearance, Giulia and the child were confined to house arrest."

I tell my mother that too much information is missing. "Please start from before Lucius Paulus' disappearance."

Scribonia sits for a moment in rare and appreciated silence. Then she continues:

"Lucius and Giulia the Younger built a lavish villa. Unfortunately, Lucius bragged about it. Your father had it razed to the ground. Then, Lucius simply disappeared. I suspect he is at the bottom of the Tiber along with the rest of the rubble. I did not think too highly of him."

Mother could be very obvious in regards to her likes and dislikes, even to the point of callousness.

"Your daughter was placed under house arrest. Augustus did not wish to encounter her. I think it reminded him of his inability to manage his own family." Scribonia passes an accusatory look in my direction and continues on. "She was accused of adultery, but everyone says the accusations were a ruse. The real reason for the punishment was Giulia the Youngers' and Lucius Paulus' lack of respect that they have shown for the *Pax Romana* and its edicts. The lavish villa was not in keeping with your father's current ideals. Incidentally, the Senate was purged immediately after this. I think he was in a foul mood. It is unfortunate that your daughter Giulia resembled you in appearance."

I interrupt my mother and plead with her to tell me about Giulia's place of exile.

"Well, I did not want to go, you understand, and be associated with these unfortunate events. It is difficult enough to stay out of Livia's sight. It is bad enough I have to come." Scribonia stopped herself in mid-sentence, stuttered and continued in a different vein. "I do not want to be banished. I hope you understand. I am too old for such inconveniences."

"Yes, I understand," I stammer, "but — I would like to hear of my daughter's plight."

Scribonia responds, "I just want to stay out of trouble's way. You ought to know how cautious I have to be. I admit I like my comforts and living in a big city, even with all its problems. I enjoy the theatre, races, and markets."

"We have a market." I reply defensively. "Once a month Damaris goes to market, and she tells me it is small but very good." I am disgusted with myself for getting sidetracked. In frustration I pound the table, surprising my mother and myself. Now I need to apologize, but I have gotten my mother's attention.

Apologizing for my outburst, I explain away my poor behaviour and tell her that I am just terribly anxious to hear about my daughter and the child.

Scribonia stiffens but acquiesces. "It is a small island just off the coast of Apulia. There are no gardens and fountains like you have here. There is just a modest house with only the bare essentials: plain utensils, a wooden table with no carvings, beds with simple woolen covers, a wood stove which is used for both heat and cooking."

"Can you imagine?" she asks, but continues not actually expecting an answer. "Some huts nearby hold scant provisions. There is a lean-to which harbours the chopped wood from the rain. There is a well. Giulia must have drawn her own water. There were no cooks or slaves that I encountered, other than a shepherd who walked me to the house. He smelled," she adds, turning her nose up in disgust. "Giulia must have received some help from the villagers. At least, I hope so."

My mother continues with a modicum of compassion. "Poor Giulia the Younger, she was always so high strung. I cannot imagine how she coped with such conditions. I guess she did not have the fortitude necessary for her seclusion. I believe it took all her strength to stay alive for Claudia's sake. She expired the day after I arrived. This has all been too much for me." Her sighs speak clearly of her inability to deal with this tragedy.

"Giulia," my mother says in a tired voice, "I am sorry I could not do more for you, your daughter and Claudia. I worry everyday about my own welfare. I am frightened for us all. It is no way to live, but I prefer it to banishment."

Embracing my mother I tell her that we both have regrets. "It is not all of our own making," I reassure her. I feel the heavy weight of her head on my shoulder.

I am relieved that my mother has left the room. I feel guilty for feeling relieved.

I need Mars the Avenger to come to my aid and deal with Livia. I visualize the statue of Mars with its muscular structure, the red-ochre disc with the dark areas that run deep like the bottom of the sea. I think that the imagery of fire and water to be contradictory. The fire symbolizes his passionate nature and the water his concern for agriculture. But vengeance will not bring back my poor dear children who are dead now just because they were my offspring. I hope I am wrong about Livia. Probably, I am not. Instead of Mars, Apollo the Tormentor surfaces to keep me imprisoned by my own thoughts.

"Why do I speak of the gods when they have dismissed me?" I ask myself, but I have no answers to such pertinent questions.

I look at the child with a sense of gratitude that she does not resemble me. She seems to be a paler version of all of us, with her plain brown hair as opposed to the dark richness of Scribonia's hair colour. Both my father and I have green eyes and sun-kissed hair. Scribonia's eyes are dark brown, while the child's eyes are hazel in colour, dotted with green speckles. I recall Marcus Agrippa's physique to be very muscular with great definition in the right places. Our children had marvelous physiques except for Giulia the Younger. I suppose that is why the child is spindly in form. Her nose is her own, not Roman at all like the rest of ours, with a cute little knob and ever so slightly upturned. I hope she does not have my mother's shrill voice. I hope she has a voice. So far she has not uttered a word.

I try in vain to recall if I have seen a female nightingale who might have stolen Claudia's voice. I truly hope that I have not encountered one and forgotten.

"Claudia," I speak her name out loud while I stroke her forehead.

XXXII

Livia, wife of Caesar Augustus, called to be a councillor of Rome

To: Damaris and company of servants

As you will realize, the benevolent nature of the Roman Empire is well known. Carpenters will arrive in the coming year and will build a swimming pool at the villa at a site suitable for such a grand undertaking.

The benevolence of my son Tiberius is also common knowledge. He has written letters of concern to Caesar Augustus lobbying for mercy in regards to Giulia. It makes me weak to think of his forgiving nature.

The Roman people are fortunate to have such a one as my dear son in their midst.

Regards, from the Palace of Caesar Augustus

Words fail me!

XXXIII

Damaris, called to be a servant of the Roman Empire

To Livia, councillor of Rome

Greetings!

We, your servants, have agreed that the building of the pool last September brought some relief to Giulia's doldrums. The kindness that comes from your household is reassuring.

We do not wish to burden you with added responsibilities, but we have not received any supplies for the past few months. Nor have we received our stipends. As we are all of meagre means and our situation is becoming dire, we appeal to you to inquire into this situation.

Thanking you in advance for your expediency.

Submitted on the kalends of June in the 3rd year of our exile.

Mishma carries this letter along with one from Giulia and another from the gatekeeper to the ship in harbour. Likely the content is similar.

    We are all surprised that the building of the pool has been so engaging and not just to Giulia. Mishma, Dilf and I have been mesmerized by the achievements of each day's work. Each one of us in different ways has been entertained by the different skills. The mixing of the cement, the turning and folding has captured my attention. Three parts gravel, one part cement, followed by the kneading, not unlike bread-making, I might add. Noticing the bulging muscles on the worker's arms, I examine my own, but all that is noticeable is dangling flab. Perhaps their arms would not be so firm if they were to sample their product as often as I am wont to do.

Now in the cooler months, the pool sits idle. This must be a relief to Mishma and his workload.

The hunger in our bellies is slowing us all down. Our stomachs churn like curdled cheese with unkindly thoughts. The Roman Empire's unmet obligation to all of us, including Giulia, causes me to lose sleep. That in turn is troublesome, since there is much to be done in a day, and we servants need our strength. Now, besides being hungry and worrying where our next meal is coming from, there is anger to deal with.

Thanks to Dilf's foraging, our meagre diet is supplemented with some mushrooms, herbs and greens. The pickings are pretty meagre this time of the year. No matter how I prepare the root vegetables, they end up tasting like dirt.

Market is ten days away. We will trade what little we have for some staples. Last month the villagers gave us some eggs, flour and dried fish. It seems they know of our plight. Their generosity makes the three of us choke with emotion. They are poor people, yet they give generously of what they quite likely cannot afford.

My letter to Livia is terse. How can it not be? I will suffer the consequences if need be. Our plight needs to be brought to attention.

All of this does not go unnoticed by Giulia. She is used to giving alms to the poor, not taking from them. The humiliation in her eyes is plain to see.

It is reassuring to see that both Giulia and the gatekeeper have written letters. I hope Caesar Augustus and Livia see the injustice of this shameful situation. They have so much wealth and the poor commoners of the village so little. It is just not right.

Enough of these thoughts! I must go and make sure that Dilf is drying the mushrooms properly. Hopefully, she has not placed them in the hot sun. They need to be dried slowly, in the shade. I try not to correct her, but then I do, and then I have to belittle myself. It is no wonder servants get tired.

Then there is laundry to be done, and without the fuller's soap! It will leave the clothing limp like my gait.

"Poor Damaris," I speak the words aloud, reminding myself that I have no time or inclination for self-pity. The spoken words bring me back to reality.

"We will have oats," I add, still speaking aloud to an imaginary presence in the room, but more cheerily now, "with dried berries and watered down milk from Dilf's wily old goat".

At tonight's meal, we will offer thanks to Dilf for her contribution. Hopefully, it will smooth over the harm done to her earlier today by a churlish taskmaster.

XXXIV

Livia, Empress of the Roman Empire

To Giulia

Might I remind you that exile means you have lost your rights as a Roman citizen.

Nevertheless, Tiberius' benevolent nature is evident in his response to your pleas. Rumour has it that an eagle snatched a piece of bread right out of his hand. The eagle flew away, and then it seems it had second thoughts, returning with the bread and dropping it at Tiberius' feet. We take this as a sign of his greatness. Many accounts of his elevated stature have been related by the people he serves so well, and the omens confirm this.

It is unfortunate that you did not believe in the power and prestige that your marriage would have afforded.

I hope that during your exile you will grow in conviction and attain some of the qualities of womanhood that have eluded you despite our best efforts.

Even though a vast endless sea separates us, Livia still has the means to agitate me to no end. I suppose the eagle incident will be repeated over and over again, just like the one and only good speech Tiberius ever made, which was at his father's funeral. I do not have a memory of it, but that is not necessary, as Livia keeps it alive, reinforcing it in the people's minds like concrete pillars.

I pray to mother earth and the Shades that we never go hungry again. It is so unfair to Damaris, Dilf and Mishma. They have not lost their rights to be treated with dignity. The little piece of bread that was dropped at Tiberius' feet was likely more than we had at some meals. Maybe the eagle in its own way was helping us out, reminding Tiberius that the allowance and wages we receive are truly no more than crumbs from the Roman coffers.

Furthermore, I have no desire to grow into womanhood and emulate Livia. It is bad enough that we who are under her guidance are encouraged to model her handwriting. I am proud that I insisted on my own distinctive style even though it caused me duress.

It seems that while ruminating on Tiberius' greatness and Livia's chastisements I have spooled a substantial amount of thread. "Good work," I say out loud to myself.

XXXV

Livia, Empress of the Roman Empire

To Damaris

Rhianis dedicated his poem to me inscribing it to Livia, Empress of the Roman Empire. What a brilliant poet he is! Now everyone has taken to my new title. I am humbled by such good fortune.

Enclosed please find your stipends. Please distribute them accordingly. Abundant supplies will accompany the funds. Poor Tiberius was not well and had to retreat to Capri to regain his strength. In the milieu some of his duties which were assigned to others were overlooked. Those concerned will be punished.

Our generosity ought to be praised. Tiberius ought to be venerated for tending to these oversights in light of his frail condition.

Good health be with you.

As I read Livia's letter a notion of incredulity washes over me.

"It is no wonder that God does not like us!" Guiltily, I look towards the heavens, but then I cannot seem to stop myself and add, "What is there to like?" As I punch the bread down, the body prayer goes unanswered. Punching and kneading helps soothe the inner conflict raging in my gut.

The prophet Isaiah says that God knows everything about us. Well, God must shake his head in despair at the miserableness of us all.

It is plain to see that I am in a truly foul mood, even taking one of my favourite scriptures and turning it into a complaint. "God knows everything about us, yet still loves us." I try to quell the bitterness as I stop the punching and the kneading. I have gone too far: the bread will be tough and course.

As for Tiberius being frail, just who does Livia think she is trying to deceive? Does she really believe her own words? He is as robust and strong as ever a man I have encountered. His mean-spiritedness and cruelty girds his loins, giving him the strength and the courage he needs to carry out his misdeeds.

Scrubbing the counter over and over in an attempt to blot out this bitterness, I then proceed to scour it with a miserly amount of soda. The supplies have finally arrived but are not yet unpacked.

Perhaps food will put me in a better mood. And maybe this dizziness will go away, and I can get on with better things like cooking with a few more ingredients.

XXXVI

"What if he throws away the key?" I ask Damaris, speaking of the gatekeeper. I worry that I might be locked in here for ever. I have mulled over several avenues of escape, but they are all hazardous. Besides, I have lost my agility. Dangling from a rope overlooking a precipice makes me dizzy just thinking of it.

Damaris smiles at me and replies, "No one ever throws away a key."

Thinking about her response, I recall a time when my porcelain lock box that held secrets and trinkets shattered when I dropped it on the tile floor. Still, I kept the key, thinking perhaps that it was a key to another box. I came across that key more than once but thought that I ought to keep it just in case it belonged to something else. Years later, my new trinket box held that same key. Damaris amazes me with her wisdom and yet, to my knowledge, she is uneducated. Or is she? I realize that I do not know very much about her.

"Damaris, where do you get your wisdom?" I ask.

Damaris tells me she is not wise, just knowing. "Sometimes I know things are right, just as you know that there is truth to be found in bread made without yeast." Damaris pauses before continuing. "As for learning, I was taught to write, but I am slow forming letters. I was taught in the ways of God. Prayer is important to me. These are the matters that are important to me."

Damaris continues on. "Being grateful instills a sense of gratitude and keeps me from harbouring resentments. I try to be a grateful person. I have a simple understanding of things that hold their own truth. I know how to cook and tend to people's needs.

"I am a woman of simple means," she affirms.

I think about the key to the villa gate. It is adorned with three carved crowns at the head. All my father's keys are carved this way. The three crowns depict Augustus' divinity, his lordship with authority over everything, and liberator, the bringer of peace. The trinity also stand for the triumvirate of Mark Antony, Lepidus and Octavian. My father was later given the title of Augustus, the illustrious one. The key is large with an intricate design. It is strong and sturdy, like the Roman Empire. It serves two purposes, and that is to keep me locked in and the world locked out. It serves its purpose well.

Here, in this place, I do not need to lock my secrets and trinkets in a box. There is no one to snoop or to take things that do not belong to them. I am indifferent to things that used to concern me. Indifference is a soothing balm to my soul. When once I took more interest in the things of this world, I now take solace in the feel of the cold marble floor beneath my feet, a rainy day and cloud formations.

Sitting on the bench that overlooks the courtyard, I finger the scar on my right leg. The scar is from a time in my childhood when Berenice, Tiberius and I were playing tag. I ran through the bush and fell. I got up and saw a sharp branch protruding from my knee. Only then did I begin to scream in pain. The injury was minor, and the scar is barely visible, but the screams can be heard over the eons.

Every scar on my body holds a memory. Here is one on the side of the back of my neck from the time I was nearly killed. My father had taken me with him to Jerusalem, against my mother's wishes, I might add. She said I was too young for such a trip. It was a long journey from Rome to Jerusalem, and I cannot recall much of it, except for our parade through the streets. I stood at my father's side, barely visible, for I was just tall enough to peer over the edge of the litter. We had a couch to sit on, but I stood stoically at my father's side for the entire route.

We stopped in front of the temple. There was a little dark skinned girl about my age who climbed the stairs, by herself, without the aid of a bannister. She proceeded to do a joyful dance that delighted the crowd. Her dance brought to mind a release of doves. Her blue cape flowed with the wind as she twirled and laughed. Initially, I was delighted, but then I became quite jealous of all the attention she was receiving. I remember tugging at my father's toga to bring his attention back to me. He laughed at me, I remember that also.

Later that day there was a violent thunderstorm. We took shelter beside a large column. I recall a streak of lightning that caused the hair on our heads to rise, followed by a loosened piece of relief from the column that grazed my neck and shoulder. Then I do not recall anything other than a bearded man who spoke a language that I did not understand. He applied a soothing ointment. My father told me it was a special balm from a place called Gilead. I remember it was reddish and very sticky. The man placed his warm hand on my forehead and uttered some words that were reassuring, even though

I knew not what he was saying. His hand made me feel better. He gave me a palm frond, illustrating how I was to fan myself. I liked it better than my fan made of exotic peacock feathers and precious jewels.

It was said that I was lucky to be alive. My father said I was stoic. I was very proud, even though at the time I did not know what the word 'stoic' meant. The augur told my shaken father that it was a portent of my indomitable spirit. I have a scar that tells the tale.

Now I have another scar, but it is not visible. I name it "Phoebe". This scar has done more damage than the other two. There is not enough balm in all of Gilead to heal this wound.

XXXVII

Berenice

To Giulia, my true friend

Greetings to you from Rome

Firstly, I have not forgotten you, and I remember you in my prayers, petitioning God for forgiveness for you and your misdeeds. I feel compassion for your predicament and share in your suffering and humiliation, as a good friend is wont to do.

I have good news to share with you. I have been betrothed to King Archelaus, son of King Herod.

When I was first introduced to Archelaus, I was bedazzled with his countenance. He was clothed in splendour, wearing a silver robe as radiant as a firmament of stars. So commanding was he, in speech and action, that I was immediately smitten. It felt like I might shatter, sending my shards along with his stardust into kingdom come.

After our marriage, we will reside in his father's winter palace, near Jericho. Then we will move into our own palace in Judea, the land that he rules over, along with the territory of Samaria. I am giddy when I relate to you that I shall become his queen.

Fortune has spread a cloak of abundance over our household.

I wish you were here to share in this excitement, and to help with the marriage plans.

Peace and grace be with you.

I come close to causing the papyrus to burst into a blazing fire as I read Berenice's greeting, addressed to her 'true friend'.

Misdeeds, indeed! Incredulous!

I sputter over my thoughts with a feeling of indignation.

I cannot say that I share in Berenice's excitement, for that would not be truthful. But I am pleased for her good fortune. I speculate that my father has his sight on a new province. Berenice would be oblivious to the political intrigue that is behind our arranged marriages.

Berenice's letter gives me a modicum of hope. Perhaps I shall be of some use, after all, when I return to Rome. Perhaps I shall be betrothed to someone in a faraway land, where people are not so informed about my 'misdeeds'.

I sit down and ponder a reply. It takes time to find authentic words that reflect my thoughts and feelings.

Giulia

To Berenice

Greetings from Pandateria

I congratulate you on your good fortune.

May your union be blessed with good health, prosperity and fecundity.

Peace Be With You.

Damaris — whose name means heifer

XXXVIII

Tomorrow, right after preparations for breaking fast, I will inform Giulia of my plans. I have put this off far too long. Over and over, I have made plans to go to her and have been prevented from doing so by my own cowardice. The problem is that I just do not know how to approach the subject. I am ill-prepared and have to get it right in my head first. First of all, I muse, I need just the right explanation, but then I do not want to appear unappreciative.

Giulia has asked Dilf and me to stay in her employment after her return to Rome. Giulia has told us that there will be no guarantees. She is not certain about her own status or financial situation. A position would most likely be made available for us in light of our good standing.

This uncertainty, along with not wanting to be considered an ill-omen because of my affliction, has helped me make a decision. Most of all, I have aspirations of dedicating my life to God, and to serving in a community by helping those with true adversities. Giulia's exile will soon be over and she shall return to her life of privilege. It is difficult for me to voice my aspirations.

It has been weeks now that I have mulled this conversation over in my head.

"Giulia," I clear my throat and practice aloud. "I have an important matter to discuss with you."

Startled, I twist my ankle, throwing myself off balance as Giulia responds, "Yes, Damaris, what might that be?"

"I did not hear you come in," I stammer. "I have made plans with Zaul, a friend, the captain of the ship that brings our provisions. I will — he will," I mumble. I am so embarrassed, it is difficult to continue. I swallow hard, "He will provide passage to Corinth. After a short stay with his friends, Prisca and Aquila, the two of us will walk to Cenchrea, six milestones from Corinth. I worry about walking so far and if I will be capable of l keeping pace with Zaul. He is bandy-legged and walks with a short stride. Perhaps, I need not worry. We will make good companions on the journey." I quickly add, "Phoebe, a deacon in the church at Cenchrea, has offered to employ me as a servant for her ministry. Zaul has made these arrangements on my behalf." I stop speaking. I have said too much, spoken too fast, and, furthermore, I am uncertain that I have explained myself clearly.

Giulia does not speak. The sadness in her eyes is palpable. I swallow spit. It sickens me to cause her any more sorrow than she has already endured these past five years.

Finally, with reticence, Giulia speaks. I can barely hear her words. "Well then, I wish you well. I am sorry. I cannot seem to find the right words to express myself. What can I say? You mean more to me than my own —" Giulia did not finish the sentence. "I mean to say, I will miss you." Giulia murmurs. It is as if her voice is drowning in the sea along with her incoherent words.

After a moment of introspection, Giulia speaks more clearly, with conviction in her voice. "Thank you, Damaris. Thank you for everything. You are a pillar. You have been our pillar."

Curiosity erases the dullness that has previously engulfed Giulia and enlivens our awkward interaction.

"This Zaul, are you and he —?"

Giulia does not finish the sentence. I quickly respond with a resounding "Oh, no, not at all. He is just a friend, and a rather young one at that, barely more than a boy. He is crass, impatient, contrary and hot-headed. Also, he is not a follower of 'The Way' and not even a God-fearer. Even if he were older, we would not be a good match. But, we are not always attracted to like-minded folk, are we? Sometimes we are drawn to another for unfathomable reasons. I might add that he seems to be amused with our unlikely friendship."

I am talking more than I desire to. Nevertheless, I continue on against my own better judgment. Our bond came the day he told me that he is not inclined to be noble, but he would see what he could do about finding passage for me, and I responded with, "That is fine with me; I am not a woman in distress, just a person in need of safe passage."

"After that exchange," I tell Giulia, "we became steadfast friends. I might add that I am not unappreciative. He has taken action and made tentative plans for me to consider."

I did not tell Zaul, nor do I tell Giulia, that I believe that it is God who provides. This would not be a topic I am prepared to discuss with either of them.

With a smile on my lips, I add, "It seems I am often drawn to those who do not share my views."

Both of us close our eyes as if this might shut out the imminent ending of our time together.

Mishma – whose name means one who hears

XXXIX

With her own hands, Giulia has woven me a linen tunic from the finest thread. The belt has a purple purse fastened to it for all my belongings. It is knotted securely with the worn thread from my father's belt. This robe is truly fit for royalty. I am humbled by such an extravagant gift.

All this finery seems to be challenging me to accept the good things that come my way. Goodness and mercy along with the scroll from Isaiah are nestled in the purse. The colour is, truthfully, more of an earthly brown than purple like an aubergine. Dilf dyed the fabric and was disappointed with her results. In my eyes, it is the richest purple ever. Damaris tells her it is just right, because I could be arrested for wearing purple, which is reserved for the nobility. Damaris always says the right thing. Dilf is now content with the results.

Damaris tells us that no one can take away the spirit of things. Once again, she is quite right. Her comment has made me aware that manhood dwells deep within, encouraging me to focus on strength and virtue. These traits were a part of my father's fabric. I hope they will become instilled in me.

Now, Giulia has called me by my name, for she has an announcement that pertains to me. I am perspiring profusely in anxious anticipation. With shaking hands, Giulia unfolds a gilded scroll from a silken tube.

Giulia reads, aloud.

To Giulia

Greetings from Queen Candace of Ethiopia

I have not forgotten you. I recall the time we met when you were a young girl. Your indomitable spirit at such a young age is memorable. You captured my attention with your animated conversation, which held wisdom beyond your years.

Your exile troubles me. I had expected the Roman Empire to profit from your gifts. It was evident that your father, Caesar Augustus, was proud of your vital spirit and had aspirations for your future role in serving the Empire of Rome.

As for your request, we will be honoured to offer the libertine, Mishma, a position in the court. Your recommendation is all that is required.

An Alexandrian ship will leave Fair Havens on the ides of May of this year. The captain will have orders to provide Mishma with a safe journey to the port of Tahpanhes. Mishma will stay at the home of Apollos, the camel trainer, and wait for a caravan that will take him to his destination in Ethiopia.

You will have to make your own arrangements for Mishma's passage to Fair Havens.

It warms my heart to receive back one of our own. It also confirms my high opinion of your good character in providing for your libertines.

Peace and grace to you

"Oh my," is all I could muster. I bow down to Giulia while kissing her hand. She is reluctant to accept this gift of servitude. It is the only gift I have to offer freely, for I am now a libertine, offering her a humble gift of gratitude.

Mixed emotions overwhelm us all. I tremble with excitement one moment and shudder with a sense of doom the next. It has been safe here on this island. Life has been predictable. We have food to eat most of the time, clothing to cover us, and work to keep our minds busy and our bodies fit.

I glance at those who have been my companions for the past five years. Damaris has been our mainstay, supporting us all through all the storms. Dilf has been the oarsmen, working diligently towards our destination. Giulia has been the castaway, struggling against the ebb and flow of the sea and finally settling into life's unpredictable patterns. Claudia is the balm we all so desperately need. Unknowingly, Claudia saved Giulia from succumbing to the black gall. Giulia had been losing her battle against the dark spirit. Her voice waned. Her breathing had become increasingly shallow. Tending to Claudia's survival diverted Giulia's attention from her own plight. After Claudia's arrival, I sensed Giulia's spirit returning with each passing day.

I cannot see what part I have played in enhancing our small community. My parents never spoke of the things they did for us and I never thought about the ways I was helpful to them. It was what we did out of love and respect for each other. Listening is my only skill. Talking tires me. Perhaps I am just a fellow voyager. I do hope I have contributed in some small way to their well-being.

It is the child who brings a lump to my throat and tears to my eyes. I shall miss her more than words can convey. I will carry with me her innocent trust, her gentle eyes, her limp little body striving to survive, and her patience when listening quietly for the birds while imitating their call. I will hold forever an image of a little outstretched hand held steadfast waiting patiently for the chickadee to light. She has given me hope that there might be children in my life, even though I am unable to have any of my own.

In a chamber of blessed silence, we convey our unconditional love for one another. The silence holds all the words that have been left unspoken and all the thoughts and feelings that have been concealed.

XL

The three of us look back on our island as we put out to sea. We wave to the islanders, and they reciprocate. We all wave and wave. I feel deceitful, like Livia must feel, since I do not have an authentic attachment to these folks, except for Dorcas. I search her out. Twisting my hands and wrists together, I hope she understands my attempt to gesture the weaving of our relationship. She gestures back. Dilf and Claudia wave enthusiastically. It does not take long before the people are out of sight, since the harbour is small and protected by land on three sides. The last place we see is the 'Villa Giulia', as it is now called by the villagers.

This ship is smaller than the one that brought us, but my memory has been dimmed by time and experience, so I cannot say this is true. The expanse of the sea is overwhelming, causing my heart to quicken. I try to rationalize my fear. Surely, my perceptions have been altered by too much time in isolation. The world appears to be much larger than I recall, but it cannot be. Perhaps it is I who is diminished. The endless expanse of the sea is frightening. I feel as insignificant as one tiny drop of water in this wretched sea. I have a peculiar feeling of wanting to turn back to the safety of my prison. I suppose I have gone mad. If not, my contrary thoughts will cause me to do so. I ought to feel elated at returning home.

Truth be known, I am panic stricken at returning to Rome and the unknown life that awaits me. Dilf and Claudia huddle on the wooden bench facing their own fears. Knowing Dilf, her memory of the passage over to this island has not been dimmed. On the voyage over, I recall privately scoffing at her lack of fortitude. Even though I am sympathetic, I am incapable of comforting them. I question when I lost my sense of bravery.

What seems like ages now becomes a reality. Apparently, we have an extended voyage. There is an important edict to drop off at various ports of call. Our first stop is the town of Rhegium. I fear we shall never get home. Then, in the next breath, I fear that we shall.

Hours later, in the fading light of day, we arrive at our first destination. We will continue on at sun up. The captain's countenance dictates that we are to be on time.

We stay overnight at the home of Olivia Procula, a kindly woman who tries to make us welcome, but who is also astute enough to leave us to our rest. None of us would be good company. Dilf is dizzy. Claudia is asleep. I am weak and unwell. I ask to be excused and retire for the night. The sparse room would please my father. It has a low bed with plain covers, a wooden desk, and an oil lamp, already lit.

Even though I am travel weary, it takes a long time for me to fall asleep. My concerns are rampant. What if my father will not forgive me? If I have to live in the women's quarters rather than my own suite, I shall truly go mad. What if Tiberius is no longer in self-imposed exile? I hope I never have to encounter him. "Never!" I spit. I have managed to wash my hands of this mad man. It has not been an easy task.

Is another husband part of their plan? I am not certain I could cope with another unwanted relationship. Will Claudia stay with me, or will Livia remove her from my care? Of all the things that trouble my weary soul, it is Claudia's care that brings the utmost anxiety.

If Damaris were with me, she would tell me that tomorrow has enough worries of its own.

She is quite right. But the memory of her words loses power without her presence.

Early in the morning, the three of us ready ourselves for the continuation of our journey. I am slightly irritated by the lack of expediency to get us back to Rome, or perhaps my impatience is a result of a poor sleep. I am both excited and terrified.

Olivia Procula sits in the corner wiping a tear from her eye. I am touched but perplexed by this display. Perhaps she is lonely. I take the time to thank her for her hospitality. She responds only with a nod.

Unbeknownst to me, I have been holding my breath. I release a huge stress-filled sigh and gird my loins. We are on our way, once again.

The pathway leading from Olivia Procula's home is littered with our baggage. "What in hell's damnation is going on here?" I cry out.

Running towards the port, I trip and fall in my haste. Picking myself up, I stare at the empty port. My eyes search the vast, empty sea in disbelief. Confusion turns quickly to anger.

With pounding heart, I turn to the sea, and then back to the town of Rhegium. As if one foot were nailed to the ground, I circle round and round.

"I do not understand. What is happening? If this is true, then bring me a dagger. I will bloody it myself."

Then I see the decree with its unmistakable Roman seal. The left wing of the waxen eagle dominates, with its sinister dark shadow, expressing an all-encompassing expanse of injustice. I stand, staring in disbelief, as I read aloud the proclamation that I, Giulia, would be held in perpetuity, in the town of Rhegium and, furthermore, without privilege to visit the city of Rome.

I read it. I re-read it. I stare in disbelief.

"Oh, these damned dreams." I laugh hysterically. I stand paralyzed, waiting for wakefulness. I stand stone still until my legs become unseaworthy, all the while pinching myself until I wince with the stinging pain of reality. I will this dream to vanish like the others.

"This is not a dream; it is a bloody nightmare!" I scream at the proclamation while slapping my face hard so that I might awaken.

"You cannot do this to me," I cry. "It is not right. It is not just. I have served my sentence, paid penance for my sins. What more do you want of me?"

Running now, but with what seems like shackles on my ankles, I make my way down to the end of the pier. The hem of my shift becomes weighted down by the sea water that has swamped the wooden platform. I sit down in a dry place for a long time until the briny stains transform into powdered white chalk. I clutch the decree that I have ripped from the post, firmly in my fist.

"I will walk then. I will take the road that leads to Rome. I will conspire with your foes to overthrow you. You hypocrites! Say it to my face, you bloody cowards."

XLI

"The ship has left without me." I utter these words over and over to myself until I accept the reality of it all.

I am to live with Olivia Procula. She is forthright informing me that she is paid to house me. Hopefully, my family is not aware that Claudia is with us. Scribonia was never informed of Claudia's survival. She never inquired about her welfare, so we thought it prudent to keep it to ourselves. Olivia has offered Dilf employment in her household. Dilf has readily accepted. I am in awe of Dilf's adeptness to accept life's transitions with a grain of salt.

I am so distraught about being abandoned that I cling to Olivia like moss to a stone. Wherever she goes, I go, following her around like a puppy. My guts roll over in anguish when she is out of sight.

Olivia treats me like a daughter ought to be treated, with respect and loving kindness. She encourages me in my spinning and weaving and sits nearby. Her presence is comforting. I have noticed that Olivia never tires and never yawns. Her energy is boundless. Olivia shares her secret. She tells me to take a nap every day, "Then you can live two days in one." Olivia laughs as she nods. This statement sends a shock of recognition. I recall this is something that Damaris would have said.

Like Damaris, Olivia believes in one god. I suppose it is one and the same as Damaris' god. I am not certain if their god is responsible for instilling in them a sense of charity. The two of them are selfless in their actions towards others. Neither of them is interested in reward. They are both gentle, yet firm in their convictions.

Olivia uses her hands in the same manner as Damaris: to serve, to pray and to help those in need. Sometimes, I hold my hand over my heart in reverence. I mimic their gestures in hopes that I will attain some of their virtue. It seems I have only succeeded in acquiring one of Dilf's habits of mimicking others. Olivia listens attentively, reminding me of Mishma. When we are in a conversation, I am made aware of her gift of being totally present. It takes time to listen, like feeding a chickadee takes time. I smile at the recollection of Mishma teaching Claudia patience and gentleness. Claudia's excitement the first time she fed the chickadee is as memorable as the feeling of the bird's feet clutching her finger that she so adeptly described — over and over. We did not tire of listening to her experience — over and over.

No one can learn to smell the way Dilf does. She can tell us a day ahead of time if it is going to rain. Dilf can sniff out mushrooms with the sense of a hungry dog.

As for me, I have learned to taste the saltiness of reality. I muse that salt is useful to enhance flavour, but once it loses its flavour, it cannot be recovered. Like the taste of bitter herbs, past regrets linger. "Faster than you can boil asparagus." My father's words come to mind as I contemplate how quickly my life has been altered.

Even though I am so fortunate to be in her nurturing care, I dream of returning to Rome. I feel a strong urge to go back to my people. I had asked Olivia to go with me, but she said that even though she understands my longing, she needs to stay with her people. Besides, she told me that she is too old for such an arduous journey.

The Procula home has become a safe haven for me. I have an abiding love for Olivia. I am made complacent by her comforting presence. Perhaps the reason for my dependence on her is guided by fear. I never used to be fearful. Now I live in fear of being separated from her and Claudia. The next moment I live in fear of smothering Claudia. I take consolation that Claudia is so well cared for by Olivia. Olivia affords her the freedom that I cannot offer.

It will take time for me to wean myself from my dependence on Olivia. I know it is an unreasonable attachment and not in keeping with my longing to return to Rome. I am being pulled in two directions.

To prepare myself, I ask the townspeople for directions to Rome, the distance and all such pertinent information. They roll their eyes, smile in a decidedly condescending way and offer directions. "Take the one and only road on the northern outskirt of town. Take one step and you will be heading in the right direction." I smile at my naiveté. I have learned to accept my limitations.

It takes longer still to work up the courage. It has been a long time since I have done anything courageous. I am aware that my level of risk-taking has become extremely restricted by my confinement. It has been ages since I have made any decisions. I desire to do these things, but mostly I just think about them.

Perhaps awareness is a beginning.

"The Road to Rhegium"

XLII

When I heard the rooster crow for the third time, I began the long walk to Rome. With each step I breathed in the fresh morning air and breathed out treasonous thoughts.

I have been informed that the journey would take seven or eight days to reach Puteoli, where I would then hire a carriage to take me the rest of the way to Rome. There is much traffic on this road, and I fear someone might recognize me, even in my altered state.

The people I pass this morning are all heading towards Rhegium. It seems I am the only one traveling in the opposite direction. This suits me fine, for I am never quite ready to converse with anyone at this ungodly time of the day.

Like the blisters on my feet, doubts surface after only three milestone markers. It is my intention to use money sparingly and wait for a few days into the journey to hire a donkey or a cart. I pat my concealed purse for reassurance. The leather thongs of my sandals are already biting viperously into the side of one foot and into the heel of the other, forcing a limp that fails to bring relief.

"Only two hundred and seventy more markers to go," I mutter. "Not yet," I chide myself, "it is too early to be so discouraged."

Damaris' voice echoes over the eons: "Like the crossing of the freed slaves at the Sea of Reeds, the real miracle lies with the person who took the first step."

The morning sun is still low in the sky. With renewed conviction, I press on, taking advantage of the coolness of the day. I am determined to make it to the tenth milestone by noon.

All too soon, determination transforms into resignation. It is well after high noon when I reach my goal. The milestone is marked by a very large purple boulder that glistens like amethysts in the sunlight. The other side is more to my liking, even though it is in tones of dull grey. Spreading my shawl on the ground, I slump down with a sigh of relief. Removing my sandals along with strips of skin stuck fast to the leather thong by congealed blood, I cry out in pain. Tiberius would delight in my squeals of weakness.

"I will never reach my destination." As usual, hunger overrules doubt, so I open the knapsack Dilf has prepared. There is a good size block of cheese, along with flatbread wrapped in linen. A small red earthen jar holds olives swimming sensually in oil. Best of all, in the bottom of the sack, I find strips of cloth along with six aloe leaves. Dilf is astute when it comes to foresight and practical things. I shake my head in approval at the amazing woman she has become.

The balm in the aloe leaf is as soothing as the cool waters of a spring brook. Audible sighs of relief escape my lips as the coolness assuages the heat of my tortured feet. I am amazed that this innocent looking salve has the ability to quell the burning sulphur of this searing pain. Tenderly, as if Dilf were actually here with her cleansing healing touch, I bind my feet with strips of cloth.

Not ready to carry on, I decide to rest for a while longer in this place of stillness. My thoughts turn to earlier in the day when I neared the eighth milestone marker. A man and a woman had joined me. Unfortunately, they did not have a donkey or a cart, but their company helped me to forget about the distance yet to be covered. We discussed the governing body of Rome. They said Caesar Augustus is more concerned with levying taxes than he is for the welfare of his citizens. "We get to do the backbreaking work while his advisors recline over banquets devising ways to milk more from us poor plebeians." The husband spoke of the long hours his family endured in order to meet the increasing demands of the Imperial treasury. It was obvious that his wife was heavily burdened, not just with long hours, but also with the pack she was carrying on her back. They both were carrying sacks of rags to sell to the landowners along the way. This was only a means to supplement their income. Most of their revenue came from corn and flax.

Fortunately, they did not recognize me. Besides, this made for more honest conversation. But why should they know who I am? I am six years older than when I left Rome. I have striven myself from signs of prosperity and dressed as a poor traveler to discourage robbers. I pat my concealed purse once again for reassurance. I doubt that even those I knew well would recognize me, for I am but a remnant of what was once a beautiful garment. Now, I see beauty differently and not as rich and ornate. It is something I see dimly, yet wont to describe. Actually, I do not mind being plain and ordinary. It is strangely comforting. Picking at my frayed hem, I surmise that to live a simple life one must choose a simple garment. I speculate as to whether my shift was made from some of their rags.

While I rest, I pose pertinent questions:

Why do I want to return to Rome?

Do I really want to be part of a treasonous plot?

Will I just be a pawn in the overall scheme of things?

If caught, what punishment awaits?

Would I be united with Antonius at the bottom of the Tiber?

Would my father ever absolve me of my past sins?

Would I even be allowed an audience, which would entail getting past Livia?

Would Tiberius remain vindictive towards me?

Even though I ponder these things in my heart, I know full well the answers. A wise person ought not to expect victory over a powerful tyrant or his scheming mother, or for that matter, an unforgiving father.

I think about Olivia and her different ways of mothering. Even though she is not overtly affectionate, I feel more accepted than I ever have. I am wont to say loved, for I have no faith in love. Love is not a feeling; it is madness. When I am with Olivia, I desire to be a better person and not for the sake of recognition or worldly honours. I am inspired by her integrity to choose the right way and the right reasons for her actions, which are mostly out of concern for others. Perhaps I shall acquire some of her ways. Perhaps Claudia will then desire to emulate my ways. That would be fulfilling.

I feel confident leaving Claudia in Olivia's care until I am settled, or perhaps forever. I fear for her well-being if she is associated with me and my treasonous plans. It seems I had to leave her in order to realize how treasured she has become. Both Olivia and Claudia are precious in my eyes. I cannot think of anyone, other than Agrippina in Rome, who carries this distinction.

Claudia has the gift of observation. Claudia is capable of blending in with her environment so adeptly that folks sometimes forget that she is present. I suppose this behaviour has been learned by keeping company with Dilf whose methods of hunting and foraging require concentration and stillness. Claudia has also learned the gift of quietude from Mishma who has a rapport with plants and birds. His skills are superior to the most respected augur who studies plants and birds for signs and omens. Consequently, Claudia listens with the keen ear of a dog. My thoughts go back to the villa and to Moonbeam. The dog's senses were amazing. He could detect someone's approach well before any of us were aware. The wagging of his tail signalled a friendly visitor while a tail between his legs indicated someone not so familiar, like the workers who came to build the pool. Perhaps Claudia is gifted with foresight and her astuteness ought not to be attributed to her hearing at all. Claudia's eyesight seems to be as sharp as a chameleons'. Dilf says a chameleon's eyes can move independently of one another, giving it an advantage over its predators. If Claudia were to come to Rome, this advantageous trait would be handy. I suspect Claudia sees more than most people. I have witnessed how she can take in an entire scene as quickly as a lightning flash. She can be still and quiet, like the silence after a thunder bolt.

When I return to Rome, I would like to share all I have learned over the past few years and consequently contribute something other than little bits of vomit to the higher goals of the *Pax Romana*. But then, I ask myself, who would listen especially when all that has been learned has come from the sea, rocks, dreams and servants."

In my mind's eye, I argue my case with conviction. From Damaris I have learned that there are different attitudes regarding serving. Her gift of servitude lies in concern for others. I sometimes think that she takes pleasure in her work. I always took servants for granted and never considered their motives or feelings. I do not suppose that her attributes could be taught. I would have to have a deeper understanding which eludes me. My conviction turns to doubt. Damaris' anger comes to mind and brings a smile to my lips. I rejoice silently in her anger, which was righteous rather than vindictive. Damaris leads by example and that is why I would have difficulty teaching Claudia virtuous ways.

From Mishma, we who are of Royal Blood, and have not learned to toil, might learn that there are different ways of working other than sweat and tears. I certainly witnessed that in his manner. What comes to mind is his slow and steady pace, working long hours which resulted in a constancy that was comforting. One could definitely learn the gift of listening, for he had a keen ear. I often wondered about his silent demeanour. After the fact, I surmise that there are two kinds of silence: external and internal, which can be used in a positive or negative way. I see his silence both as light and darkness, gift and detriment.

Mishma has good reason to succumb to the darkness, and yet, despite adversity, he has chosen dignity and courage over anger and bitterness.

I am reminded of the Roman legend that my father told to the masses to promote the *Pax Romana*. He told the story of two wolves that are fighting inside us. One wolf is angry, bitter and treasonous. The other wolf is peaceful and brave. This wolf pledges allegiance to his country. Someone from the crowd, likely seeded by my father's devotees, cried out, "Who wins?" My father proclaimed, after an appropriate amount of silence, for his timing was impeccable, "the wolf who wins the battle is the one you feed."

Dilf offered different ways of healing. Even though she is knowledgeable in medicinal cures, it is her healing touch that comes to mind. I envision her bony hands, fingernails permanently embedded with dye and dirt, preparing a poultice for Mishma. I hope never to forget how these servants cared for one another and for Claudia's and my well-being.

My speech is over. I have influenced no one but myself. I see clearly that I would not be in a position to contribute to the betterment of Roman society. Ironically, it has taken the insular circumstance of exile to make sense of the worldly view of the *Pax Romana*. My chance to make a difference is no longer an option. I think how difficult it must have been for my father trying to implement the virtues of the *Pax Romana* when he had so little influence on his own family. I am sorry for the humiliation I caused him, but it is too late to make amends. My apology would fall inertly, like a seed on one of his newly paved roads.

Upon my return to Rome, I see myself relegated to the women's quarters, or bartered off to someone whose importance would be enhanced by allegiance to the Roman Empire or worse yet, rotting in the filth at the bottom of the Tiber. I see myself trying to prove that I have changed my ways while providing proof that I have not.

Like a thief who comes in the night to rob us of our belongings along with our sense of safety, a reoccurring dream steals my thoughts. I dismissed the dream because I did not want to reflect on my painful abandonment at Rhegium. In the dream, I was dressed in a royal purple robe. The salt stained hem became heavy-laden with chains. I was struggling to walk on a distant shore. I could go no further. A washerwoman came along and removed my garment. She scrubbed it with fuller's clay. The salt stains along with the purple dye were absorbed by the soap. The washerwoman dressed me in a humble robe the same colour as the buff clay. Even though the hem was ragged, I did not mind. I no longer cared about the disapproval or approval of others. That is all I recall about the dream. The augur once told me that if you have a reoccurring dream there is more to be gleaned from it. I thought about this for a while. The only thing that came to mind was the words: 'To live a simple life, a person must choose a simple robe.' "I really could use the wisdom of the augur to help me with the interpretation." I spoke the words out loud for only myself to hear.

Standing up straight, I shake my shoulders and proclaim, "I choose to return to my new home with Olivia and Claudia. I hereby denounce the people in Rome who cannot or will not embrace me. Furthermore, I denounce all retributions that I hold towards others in my own heart." "As best I can," I add, for I have come to understand some of my undesirable traits and the challenge of overcoming them.

Even though painful, this journey has been a revelation after all. I pat the shady side of the huge boulder, while running my hands over its coolness. I glance distrustfully at the reflective light on the shimmering sunny side. I pick up a stone. I am surprised as it has a clear impression of the goddess Adiona who protects a child's first steps. The simplistic white outline on the black stone shows a mother cradling a child. I have seen this image in the hall of Roman gods. This stone is a visible reminder that I am to take possession of my own inheritance. I suppose the gods have not abandoned me entirely. I place the stone in my pocket. Hopefully it will be a reminder of this day.

With purpose-driven conviction, I retrace my steps to Rhegium.

XLIII

I stop at the milestone marker just a short way outside of Rhegium. I stop to take a breath and look up. High above a cedar tree I see an eaglet dangling from its mother's pinions. I recognize this as its first flying lesson. I've witnessed this before. This time, I feel hopeful that the chick will not flounder. I recognize freedom in the eaglet's trustfulness, like I have always known this truth, but have temporarily forgotten. I see clearly the essence this liberty would bring. It is not just a dim recollection. It is a truth felt deep within. This sighting is yet another affirming omen. It instills in me the recognition that I am capable of making right decisions. It affirms that no one can take a person's inner freedom away.

"I choose to trust that I am capable of achieving these lofty goals." I speak the words to the eagle and its' young.

I approach Olivia and ask her permission to make her home my home. Olivia readily agrees. Claudia was not aware that I had left. It seems to me that Dilf expected my return. She did not appear excited to see me, as one might, after such a long journey. Then I realize I was only gone for a day. In essence it seemed much longer.

I make a promise to Olivia that I will never leave her again, that I will stay with her and that her people will become my people. The people of Rhegium know Olivia to be a noble woman, which is something I desire to emulate. She treats everyone with equal respect. Olivia has moral convictions, which she naturally lives by. In appearance she is modest, yet she always looks elegant. My father would admire her countenance. Perhaps I could at the very least acquire some of her traits.

"Wash and perfume yourself and put on your best clothes," Olivia smiles while commanding me. "There is someone I would like you to meet."

I do as I am told, for I resolve to trust her implicitly. Besides, her excitement is infectious.

****

If this were a script in a play, the next scene would be criticized for its metaphorical inadequacy. "A legionnaire in dazzling armour!" you would exclaim while throwing corn. My roberant cheeks burn with embarrassment. As truth most often is, it seems unbelievable.

Here lies the truth.

One day, not that many months ago, Olivia's son, Vitellis, returned to Rhegium from a posting at the Roman Colony of Gaul where their cavalry was sent to keep the peace and order of the *Pax Romana*. After a successful venture and after twenty year of service, Vitellis was honoured. In appreciation for his service, he will serve his final five years, closer to home, here in Italy.

I believed I was too old and jaded to be smitten. Not that long ago, I declared to Dilf, "no more dogs and no more husbands!" Dilf choked on my words while she laughed. So much for my intentions! I suppose a person cannot foresee what fortune or misfortune lurks around the corner. This legionnaire of the equestrian order, clothed in muscular armour, causes me to have a skin orgasm. If the breast plate is any indication of what lies beneath, I am a happy woman.

Arrangements are made. We are betrothed. He will adopt Claudia and raise her as his own. Furthermore, my dearest companion shall become my mother-in-law.

The powers that be in the Roman Empire would deem this an unsuitable match, for there is no power or prestige to be gained by our union. I tell myself that those performers left during the second act.

There is simply too much happiness in the third act. I really enjoy shocking Dilf with my wicked humour, which seems to be returning. Once again she reacted with gleeful horror to my comment when I told her that too much happiness causes constipation.

If the third act is inadequate, corn will be thrown at the actors.

And yet, I dare to ask you to enter into the spirit of the performance and be pleased with the outcome, at least for the sake of the child.

Vitellis' mother delivers her lines with eloquence, "Even though at my age, when I had grown accustomed to an empty house, I find that now it is filled to the brim. Whoever said that blood is thicker than water does not understand that water can be made into the finest wine."

I deliver my lines: "Can I be content with a happy ending? Will the audience be content if there is a happy ending?"

The legionnaire leaves the stage in a flourish after delivering his final words "Peace and grace be with you."

The audience will not be fooled by propaganda, but they can be fuddled by truth. Murmurings and muttering abound.

I cannot discern if they are pleased or dissatisfied. But I am satisfied with the ending and it is my play.

Dilf – whose name means buttercup

XLIV

Never have I experienced such emotions! I exclaim.

With a wicked grin, Giulia good naturedly replies to my outburst, "When I was young, these feelings were all too frequent."

Blushing with embarrassment, I divert the conversation to Giulia, chiding her for swearing to never again marry. Now, here she is betrothed to Vitellist Procula.

"'Never' is a shallow word with an even shallower meaning," we chime in unison, echoing Damaris' words. Even though she is no longer with us, her wisdom remains.

Damaris is quite right because never would I have imagined sitting here, in the threshing room with Giulia, separating the wheat from the chaff, while discussing our forthcoming marriages. Giulia smiles at me. I smile back, mirroring our happiness.

Giulia calls the chaff by name as she tosses it to the wind. "Dilf," she says, "these vipers are like a passing breeze that shall not return." "Tiberius, Livia," Giulia tosses their names along with the dross to the wind.

The stalks of wheat are saved, for they will be made into straw. With a winnowing fork, we separate the grain from the husks.

Giulia declares "the chaff that does not blow away will be burned. With emphasis she adds, "in the fiery furnace of hell."

Amidst laughter and banter, we ready the grain that will be ground into flour. This will be made into bread that will be served on our wedding day. It will be a gift from my husband and me for all those who attend our banquet.

Giulia tells me that it is a benevolent gesture and a portent of an enduring union. She says that people will remember our marriage every time they come to market and breathe in the aroma of our bread.

John, the baker soon to become my husband, is a kindly man, more content than happy. He teases me and tells me that too much happiness causes air bubbles in the bread dough. And I tell him, that it also causes constipation. The memory of our laughter lingers in my heart.

When I first met John, it was the wafting smell of yeasty air that drew me to his stall. The aroma reminded me of the baker and his wife from the island of Pandateria. John was flattered and assumed it was the aroma of his bread. Truthfully, it was fond memories that were enticing.

I breathed in so deeply that John told me that watching me was a prayerful experience.

"Blasphemer," I whispered for only him to hear. He laughed at my retort and gave me a piece of warm bread from his portion. We ate together, savouring each bite. I remember this encounter in detail, like it happened yesterday. It is ingrained in my heart, which at the time betrayed me, thumping so wildly against my chest that I was certain he could hear it.

John is a resourceful man, as well as brilliant. He built his own clay oven with a dome that resembles a bee hive. Incised lines make it appear even more-so. He coated the red earthenware clay with yellow ochre, the colour of egg yolks. In keeping with Roman innovation, the arch of the oven and the fire-pit has been reinforced with hard fire brick.

This is not common knowledge, but he used horse urine to manipulate the wet clay, making it easier to shape. While the clay was still wet, holes were poked in the base with straw that served as rebar for reinforcement. According to John, when the straw became dry, the air pockets kept the whole thing from being blown to smithereens on the first firing. The base has a cave- like structure for firewood. Both the grate for the oven and the firewood are made of iron with the same enduring strength as the Roman Empire. With each firing the oven becomes stronger.

I wish I could have helped with the building of the oven. It seems to me that it is a remarkable example of the highest workmanship. Also, it is pleasing to the eye.

I am thinking that besides our union, the ultimate pairing would be freshly baked bread with a dollop of wild honey.

1. Aesthetic - pertaining to a sense of beauty;
2. Concerned with emotion and sensation as opposed to intellectuality

XLV

The entrance to our house is beautiful yet simple in design, with a colonnade consisting of only eight Doric columns, four on each side. A pergola with draped grape leaves provides shade, not to mention fodder for a decent snack. The grapes are small, but delicious. Olivia and I often pick them ourselves, leaving our fingernails stained with blue-black ink. This is not a bad thing, since it gave us an excuse to visit the aesthetician. Olivia prefers to support our local merchants, often abstaining from purchasing exotic goods from the caravans. I miss her immensely even though she remains a constant companion in my mind's eye.

Our home and gardens give me a sense of pride. This is baffling because our home is so ordinary. Vitellis and I are in the midst of chaos at the moment, building a bath house that overlooks the sea.

Hurriedly, I leave for the house of Joseph, the potter, for I have a pressing task. The market is not far from our house. I never tire of the walk. Each step is paved with freedom. This is something I do not take for granted. Barely noticing my favourite tree, I promise myself to stop on the way home. Out of habit, I glance up to see the branches reflecting golden light in the morning sun, causing the sky behind its branches to appear deeper blue than the rest of the sky. The contrast of the uppermost branches to the old and withered trunk is remarkable. Most days, I would stop and rest for a while. Further along, past the villas, the houses become simpler in design. There is a sense of pride of ownership evident in the neat and well cared for dwellings, even though they are austere. They are small yet strong houses, built out of volcanic matter with rubble to strengthen the concrete. I suppose our home seems opulent in comparison.

The pedestrian passage to the market is marked by a wide arched gateway made of brick and mortar. Apparently, my father's influence in architecture has no boundaries. The marketplace is the heart of our town. The street is wide and paved with stones of various shapes and sizes. Two storey buildings with balconies overlook the outdoor space. The shops are on the main level with the vendors' living quarters above. We have all kinds of shops at our market, but only one of each. We have a fabric shop, an aesthetician, an apothecary, a barber shop, a jeweller, laundry, bakery, cafe, scriptorium, et cetera. The farmers set up their stalls along the way. At the end of the street there is a blacksmith and a tavern, behind which is an arena for cockfights and a place for the men to play dice. The women cannot gamble here, nor are they allowed to attend the cockfights. My lust for such things has diminished, so I really do not mind. Ironically, I prefer to weave, which Tiberius once said does not challenge the intellect. I beg to differ, but not today, since I am not in the mood to argue with my absentee nemesis. Our market certainly is not as grand as the one in Rome, but it is adequate. We have what we need to meet our basic needs.

Crushed shards line the path to Joseph's pottery shed. The crunching sound of the broken clay beneath my sandaled feet triggers a memory from long ago. The auger had told me once that there are times when the mother eagle must coax a reluctant eaglet from its nest by lining the nest with broken and sharp pottery shards. I recall wondering why the mother is so eager to have its young leave the safety of its nest. A twinge of guilt spiders down my spine. At the time, the piercing eyes of the auger spoke clearly that I was to keep my mouth shut and not ask questions. One always knew when it was time quietly to absorb his words.

Walking through the open door, I see pots perched, like statues, on its lintel. I stand quietly while watching the potter concentrate on forming a bowl. He bites his lower lip; his eyebrows are knit together in concentration, as he skillfully draws up a cylinder, while kicking his foot on a foot-operated lever, to keep the wheel in motion. This potter's wheel is more innovative than any I have seen in Rome. He places one hand outside the cylinder and to keep a steady hand, he places his elbow firmly against his inner thigh. With his right hand inside the cylinder, he magically forms a rounded, uniform bowl. The potter continues shaping and smoothing the bowl with such precision that even Ovid would have been amazed by this metamorphosis.

I would have liked to continue watching him, but, all too soon, with his head still downcast, he raises his eyes to meet my gaze.

"What?" he demands. His voice is like a trumpet, startling me. I stand at attention. It seems he converses more with bodily gestures than with words. I suspect he would make a good lover. I chide myself and think demurely, if I were so inclined.

"I would like to purchase a wedding gift for a friend," I reply.

Joseph casts his eyes in the direction of a shelf filled with fired wares. The hardened wares appear to contain the intensity not only of the fire, but of the potter, as well.

There is much to consider in choosing the right gift for John and Dilf. I eventually choose four bowls and four cups. Then I spot a large platter, which would be perfect for their bread. The clear glaze reveals the true essence of the earthen clay. I turn the wares over and notice the potter has put as much care into finishing the product as he did in forming it. I am satisfied that this useful gift will be as noble as one made of gold or silver.

In the back of the potter's shed, a kiln is partially opened to reveal wares made strong and hard by the firing. The kiln is not so different from Dilf's and John's oven, I muse. If their marriage possesses the quality of all that goes into the making of this pottery, then they will be blessed, indeed.

We complete our transaction. Joseph's son will deliver the purchase later in the day.

Reluctantly, I leave the potter's shed. I would have liked to stay awhile longer and watch the master potter work his miracles. But his eyes, not unlike the eyes of the augur, indicate it is time for me to take my leave. As I go, I muse that the shards along the path are useful, even though they are broken. They are pleasing to the eye as well as to the ear. I walk slowly aware that I am contributing to paving the path.

At the open air café, my thoughts turn once again to the eagle and its young. I need to leave this for tomorrow, I sigh to myself, for today has been such a good day, and tomorrow holds worries of its own. Olivia once told me that a person needs to savour the times that bring consolation. I kiss two fingers in respectful remembrance of my mother-in-law.

I turn my focus to the beet root salad on my plate. The presentation is pleasing. Arranged artfully on the plate and nestled in a variety of greens are three crispy fried breaded rounds of cheese, deep ruby red pickled beets, sprinkled with white-as-snow goat cheese and strategically placed black olives. Shredded carrots, which have become a favourite food, top the salad. The colours delight the eye, while the flavours excite the palette. Epicurus was right: 'pleasure is the highest good'.

I spend a moment in gratitude for such a good day. Olivia says that even if I do not pray, I could spend a moment being thankful. I kiss my fingers, once again. At the time, Dilf overheard our conversation and added that it instills a sense of gratitude. I am intrigued at Dilf's way of absorbing trifling bits of conversation by stating the obvious. At this moment, I am grateful for the salad, particularly the crispy cheese rounds, which I savour, leaving one for the last bite.

On the way home, I stop and rest on a marble bench placed under the favoured tree. Missing bark indicates to me that Dilf has been here to collect a piece for her 'willow bark tea'. I will take the tea to the woman who makes our cheese as she has been suffering with swollen and painful hands. Thoughts which I had hoped to save for tomorrow impose upon my satisfactory morning. Images of pottery shards, an eaglet and a nest swirl around in my mind, forcing me to consider that which I do not wish to face.

I have vetoed writing Livia a letter requesting harbour for Claudia. I do not want to expose Claudia to the close scrutiny that would come with living in the Imperial household. My intention is to send her to Rome so a suitable match can be arranged for her now that she is almost thirteen years old and of marriageable age.

I have questioned whether I might ask Claudia herself of her wishes but have decided against it, since she is too young to make such important decisions. A twinge of the injustice causes the hair on my neck to quiver like the leaves of an aspen. Physically, I can feel history repeating itself. Old enough to marry but not old enough to make decisions: this is the way it is and always has been for women in the Roman Empire. I justify the decision to have her return to Rome by reflecting on the young men of Rhegium that might be suitable. They are too few and not suitable for a woman of her station. I have witnessed the way young Probus looks at her. He is very handsome but rather dull. Soon enough, her vibrant mind would grow dim with misuse. I worry that she will end up caring for me or for Vitellis. Even though he is a wonderful husband, he is still needy. And so am I, but this is the choice we made. We look out for one another. I do not wish to have her wings clipped by servitude. I believe she needs the higher ground of seven hills, where the air is more plentiful.

I visualize Claudia next door with several children, doing her own laundry, her hands red and chapped. There would be no time for poetry, no evenings at the theatre, no augers to help her interpret omens and dreams, no games or professional entertainment with trained musicians. Of course they have all this here, I remind myself, but the comedy here is course and bawdy, not humorous at all, with amateur performers who do their best. I sometimes think they get more enjoyment out of their own performance than the audience receives from their plays. Of course, many times I have found myself laughing along at their antics. The plays are rarely stimulating. It is a good thing my father has not witnessed some of the entertainment. He once had Hylas, the pantomime actor, scourged after a poor performance. I cringe with the memory of it. I cringe because it now causes me pain to think of the harsh punishment, and I cringe with shame because at the time I shivered in gleeful terror.

I want Claudia to experience the best of life, to walk on newly paved roads, and to become betrothed to a man who wears weasel pelts and recites works from literary masters. "I want her to stay right here," I cry out to the tree, "in the safety of my sheltered wings." I weep over things that have not yet come to be.

I certainly know how to ruin a perfectly lovely day. I wipe an errant tear that travels down my cheek that is in search of wisdom. Walking back to our villa, I stray from the shortest route and return a different way.

I will deal with this tomorrow.

XLVI

My legs are aching. I am ever so tired. I have decided to write my daughter. The letter to Agrippina was more taxing than I anticipated. Claudia has more strength in spiritual matters than I do, thanks to Olivia, who shaped her values more by example than by pontificating. I have encouraged this. I do not want Claudia to follow in my superstitious ways, which are tainted with cynicism and disbelief in the gods with whom I continue to make bargains. Acknowledging my shortcomings frees me from imposing my beliefs, or lack thereof, on others. This in turn frees me to celebrate the gifts others have offered me. Olivia's ways are not to be forgotten. Small shifts in thought have led me to a gradual incline in demeanor. This, believe me, surpasses the flat landscape I inhabited while in exile. I suppose my intuition is worthy of acknowledging since I have accepted the inevitability of my passing from this life into the next. Perhaps it is the increasing chest pains, rather than intuition, that lead to such speculation. With Olivia's passing came insight into the recognition that now it is Vitellis and myself who are the elders. The body declines while the spirit inclines. Such is life.

In my waning years I have been blessed with a loving family: a mother-in-law whom I unabashedly admired, a husband who is strong yet compassionate, a grand-daughter who is cherished and loving in return, a strong and supportive community, and the fading of painful memories of past harm that become more vague with time.

Rhegium is a beautiful place to live, with things that are pleasing to the eye. An abundance of magnolias and sophisticated bronze statues unashamedly attests to its Greek origin. Whenever I desire, I roam outside our gates breathing in the fresh air of freedom. Imprisonment has a way of making a person aware of incidental benefits taken for granted by most.

One can easily imagine the splendid place this will become. Growth is already evident. I see Rhegium's progressive leaders breaking with past traditions that have kept it stagnant. A promenade is being built down by the harbour with newly planted palms lining the pathway. Of course, there has been opposition to this supposed ostentatious display. The promenade has been opposed for what is deemed an unnecessary and extravagant expenditure. The plebeians discuss who might have the time to stroll for the sake of strolling. I have no doubt their opposition will be forgotten when they experience the usefulness of such a wide walkway. They might even come to understand the positive impact of culture and beauty and how it not only enhances the appearance of a community, but also instills a sense of pride in their own place. Fortunately, many in the community are in favour of enhancing the beauty of this place, and consequently the project will move forward. Many supporters promote the project and remain adamant in spite of angry opposition, especially in regards to the Palm Trees. In the end, we, who have the means, pledged our own funds for the trees. I am proud that this resolution has come from Vitellis and me. I think it would be an unnecessary burden on the taxpayers.

I understand now the importance of enforcing the edicts of the *Pax Romana*. "Too little, too late," I flippantly chastise myself. Considering all that has come to be, I am not as filled with remorse over my salacious incidents as I once was. It is more important to enhance the lives of others less fortunate than ourselves than to spend our precious time on regrets. To make life a little more peaceful and beautiful will do no harm.

There is currently an animated conversation in regards to the building of a university. I do not think this will come about for many years, but the seed has been planted. The required arguments and discussions will have to happen first. If and when it comes to fruition, cultural life will flourish. Unfortunately, it will be too late for Claudia, for all too soon youth surrenders to middle age like summer relinquishes to autumn.

I sit quietly and re-read my letter to Agrippina.

Your mother, Giulia

To: Agrippina, my dear daughter

Greetings from Rhegium

Grace and Peace to you, your husband, Germanicus and your children: Agrippina, the younger, Drusilla, Livilla, Nero, Drusus and Gaius Caesar, and in remembrance of your three sweet children.

I yearn to see you. For now, I will have to settle for fond memories. I particularly remember your intelligence and orderly ways.

After the death of your sister Giulia the Younger, her daughter Claudia came to live with me while I was in exile at Pandateria. After I was banned from Rome for perpetuity, I came to live in Rhegium where I remain in exile. Subsequently, my husband Vitellis Procula and I adopted Claudia as our own beloved child. Claudia is now thirteen years of age. As she is now of a marriageable age, we think the opportunities in Rome would be more suitable for a person of her station.

I am asking that the way might be opened for her to come and live with you and experience life that is only available in a city as vibrant as Rome.

Claudia is strong in spiritual intuition. She is quiet, perhaps to a fault, but not of her own making. Her observational skills are keen. She is always willing to lend a helping hand.

We appeal to you and your family to welcome her into your household.

I write this request in my own hand, without a wax seal.

I extend my love to you and your family.

XLVII

Your daughter Agrippina

To my mother, Giulia

Greetings from Rome

I also long to see you, but it is best you are nestled in a safe haven, free from the oppressive forces here in Rome. Agrippa has been sent into exile on the island of Planasia. My brother has no control, speaking every thought without considering the consequences. Two recent incidents likely taxed Tiberius' patience. Firstly, he poked Tiberius in the belly, pointedly gesturing to his expanding girth. Then he complained when more wine was poured into Tiberius' goblet than his own. Imagine the gall! His bad temper has been a burden to our family that only he can carry. It was likely more Agrippa's irritability than his callousness that provoked Tiberius. Regardless, I regret having to send you this news about your son.

Thank you for the compliment regarding my disposition. The most intelligent act I might do is to stay out of Tiberius' sight. He only needs the slightest provocation to punish people, his family included, as you well know. He grows more devious and suspicious of others with time. Fortunately for me, I remain in Livia's favour.

We will be pleased to accept Claudia into our household.

Only yesterday, while taking a stroll, a ship was headed pointedly in our direction. I quipped that good tidings will be coming our way.

I shall look forward to sharing the gleanings from my studies with Claudia. These words from the book of Ecclesiastes come to mind:

"What has been, will be again, what has been done, will be done again." Taking this into consideration, I believe that you might find solace in the fact that Claudia might get the opportunity afforded her that was taken from you. You might also enjoy hearing that I 'borrow' books from Tiberius' library. Please do not worry yourself. Tiberius spends months in self-imposed exile, and I am vigilant about not sharing this with anyone. It pleases me to reveal this secret to you.

I am sending this correspondence through Domitian, who can be trusted implicitly. You might do the same.

We will do our best to find passage for Claudia before winter.

Grace Be With You.

vitality – n. 1. Liveliness, animation
2. The ability to sustain life, vital power
3. the ability to endure and to perform its functions. [Latin – Vitalus]

XLVIII

I am dozing in bed with my former husband, Marcus Agrippa. Reclining on nearby couches are my father, my sons Gaius, Lucius and others who are all deeply engaged in conversation. I cannot hear what they have to say. I am distracted by the visual wonders of the lavishly presented sumptuous feast. Suddenly, rebels break into the room. They are poised with daggers, about to murder my father and sons and cut them into little pieces. Others with them are smashing beautiful works of art and overturning tables laden with wondrous displays of food. I holler out a warning to my father and sons about the dangers at hand.

I awaken with a start, my heart pumping like a reed organ. The dream provokes thoughts from long ago, which stay with me like a scar. I recall, days before I was exiled from Rome, rebels barking out their warnings of doom and gloom with words similar to the dream. "Death will come like a thief in the night, when you least expect it, like a woman's labour pains." I remember this because their arrest came as quickly as their description of Rome's downfall. I cannot help but think that these words aptly apply to my own predicament.

I gather that this dream is about my imminent death. Well, I will not be caught like a thief in the night, because I am ready to give up the ghost. The only surprising twist is that I have lasted this long. In some ways it has been a privilege to grow old. In other ways it has been a living hell.

Only yesterday, I was contemplating with interest the changes to my aging body and mind. I forget names, even those I ought to remember. I lose thoughts, not to mention pubic hair. My breasts droop while groping for the safety of my armpit. My midriff, thickened years ago, now leaves patterned folds like striations in the sand. My upper lip is much longer than it used to be. What was once a voluptuous figure has now formed into a work of art: not boring at all, but interesting in a macabre sort of way. What is not interesting, at all, is the constant fatigue. Like a baby, I have taken to napping several times a day.

Now, instead of noticing my ever-changing body, I am taking notice of my final days with a sense of gratitude for the things that bring contentment. It is difficult for me to hold a thought, and so I drift from one to the other. Dilf once said, with all sincerity that in the end life leads to death. Her common-sense approach brings profound simplicity to the simply profound. My thoughts drift to Damaris and some of her ways that I have tried to emulate, mostly unsuccessfully. She has tried to teach me to ponder instead of brood. Most of the time, I was too impatient. She taught me to amble instead of hurry. If I desired her company, which I did, I had to acquire this method. Sometimes it was revelatory, sometimes not. Most of all, she has taught me to forgive by forgiving me.

My heart flutters and not in a romantic way. I try to restore it to its natural rhythm by breathing slowly in and out. I hold fast to Vitellis' hand and notice that his hand grows deeper red while mine pales in comparison.

I reflect on what a good person Vitellis is. He not only adopted Claudia but treated her as his own. He is kind and gentle like his mother. That is a compliment of the highest order. Without Olivia, I suspect I would have gone mad. She has been my 'Naomi'. Hopefully, I have been her 'Ruth'. Damaris has shared many tales of women from ancient times in her treasury of stories. I have paid little attention to this one, until I came to call Olivia's home. It was then I gleaned the meaning of the story. Ruth, Naomi's daughter-in-law said she wanted to die where Ruth died and be buried where Ruth was buried. I understand this now, but thought it peculiar at the time of the telling. I treasure both Olivia and her son Vitellis in my heart. It comforts me to know that this will be my final resting place.

Now my mind drifts to Gaius, who did not have the privilege of growing old, raising a family and becoming Emperor of Rome. A life unlived is so unfair, but then I have learned that life is not always fair. I would have traded places with him, if allowed to do so. Others who did not get to live their lives float through my mind like cherubim freed from their stone pedestals.

Memories and images grow dim and escape me like elusive dreams. I try to tell Vitellis that I have found peace, and that this is a luxury that I have never experienced before. I am uncertain whether the words surfaced.

The quietness of this place enfolds me.

I whisper in Vitellis' ear, "*Pax*, my dear husband, to all those dear to your heart, and to all those who have no peace".

> *An eagle swoops down with a scroll and reads words uttered in my father's voice: "Since the play has been so good, clap your hands. And all of you dismiss us with applause".*

THE END

AFTERWORD

The protective spirits of a particular location are known as 'Genii Loci'.

Like the amniotic fluid that surrounds a baby in the womb, the protective spirits on the island of Pandateria hold a memory from a time of exile that cannot be banished.

Like professional mourners, the sounds from the sea echo Giulia's cries of grief. If you sit on the moss covered steps, leading to the cistern, you can taste her salty tears on your own lips.

If you follow the path into the bush of the surrounding countryside, you might hear Dilf's footsteps walking gingerly so as not to disturb or harm the delicate foliage. You might even lick your lips in anticipation of the taste of a juicy ripe berry, straight from the branch. Please, do not eat the mushrooms, unless you are certain they are edible.

In the kitchen, the walls will creak and groan, since they still hold the hustle and bustle of this room. Breathe in the yeasty smell of bread, still evident, embedded deeply into the bricks of the clay oven.

In the garden, you will never hear, but you will vividly sense Mishma and Claudia waiting silently with outstretched palms. You might experience the chickadees alighting, if you have patience. Just hold your palm upright and stretch your arm out as far as possible, all the while being careful not to move, not even when the bird lands, for any movement will frighten them.

You will find perfect stillness in Damaris' cave. It will fill you with a sense of peace only found in a place that has heard countless prayers and experienced heartfelt devotion.

Over the eons these sounds and sensations have merged with the splashing sound of the sea and have become deeply embedded within the crumbling walls of the villa. All that remains is a rock solid foundation.

Not trusting in your senses, soon enough you will shake it all off and think you imagined it all.

INFLUENCES

II

(Several Dictionaries)   Purge (purj), v. & n.
    1. make physically or spiritually clean
    2. remove by a cleansing process
    3. rid an organization of persons regarded as undesirable
    5. empty the stomach by inducing vomiting (C.O.D.)

XI

"It was in these fields, that I learned how to knock birds out of the sky with a slingshot, to gather wild honey and fruits and edible roots, to drink warm sweet milk from the udder of a cow, to swim in clear cold streams, and to catch fish with twine and sharpened bits of wire." (N. Mandela)

XVIII

["It Is Well With My Soul" Hymnist: Horatio Spafford composed by Philip Bliss After a collision with a sea vessel, all four of Spafford's daughters were lost at sea. After passing near where his daughters had died, Spafford wrote the hymn.

XIX

[And her place knows her no more] from the author's dream journal

XXI

Damaris' prayer: Anglican Book of Prayer

XX111

Inspiration from a family story by Ainy Mohammed

XXV

["Romulus and Remus" as told by Virgil
And retold by Tom White, "The Wolf Cubs"]
And retold by the author

XXVII

Inspiration: Wendel Berry; Edwina Gateley; Julian of Norwich

XXIX

(Thoughts on grief – inspired by L.Fish)
(Thoughts on weaving – inspired by MaryBelle Powers)

XXX

(A still small voice) N.I.V. Bible

XXXII

(inspiration from the poem "'Abou ben Adam"

XLII

(Credit: Thalia Took, for information on Adiona)

XLIII

Book of Ruth; NIV Bible

XLVIII

"Death will come...".1 Th 5:1-3 NIV Bible, Book of Ruth; NIV Bible Suetonius, "Lives of the Caesars" (Augustus 99) (quote by Menander)
*Several of the chapters: Suetonius, "Lives of the Caesars" (Augustus and Tiberius)

ACKNOWLEDGEMENTS

Thank you to Mary Seiferling for guiding me through the nuances of the writing world. She provided me with encouragement along with her editing expertise.

Any errors are due to my oversight and not her expertise.

Thank you to Rae-nel Trogi for her computer skills.

Thank you to Jack, my late husband, for support and encouraging me to step into the unknown territory of the publishing world.

Printed in Canada